SEDUCTION

RED STONE SECURITY SERIES

Katie Reus

Cover art: Jaycee of Sweet 'N Spicy Designs

Publisher's Note: This is a work of fiction. Names, characters, places, and incidents are either the products of the author's imagination or used fictitiously, and any resemblance to actual persons, living or dead, or business establishments, organizations or locales is completely coincidental.

Sinful Seduction/Katie Reus. -- 1st ed.

ISBN-13: 978-1497447868
ISBN-10: 1497447860

For my readers. Thank you for loving the Red Stone Security world as much as I do.

Praise for the novels of Katie Reus

"Sinful, Sexy, Suspense... Katie Reus pulls you in and never lets go."
—*New York Times* bestselling author, Laura Wright

"Has all the right ingredients: a hot couple, evil villains, and a killer action-filled plot. . . . [The] Moon Shifter series is what I call Grade-A entertainment!" —Joyfully Reviewed

"I could not put this book down. . . . Let me be clear that I am not saying that this was a good book *for* a paranormal genre; it was an excellent romance read, *period.*" —All About Romance

"Reus strikes just the right balance of steamy sexual tension and nail-biting action....This romantic thriller reliably hits every note that fans of the genre will expect." —*Publisher's Weekly*

"Explosive danger and enough sexual tension to set the pages on fire . . . fabulous!" —*New York Times* bestselling author, Alexandra Ivy

"Nonstop action, a solid plot, good pacing and riveting suspense..."
—*RT Book Reviews (4.5 Stars)*

CHAPTER ONE

Blue smiled when he saw Zoe's picture on his caller ID. The photo was from last year's Halloween party and she was dressed like a pirate. She had a patch over her eye and was toasting the camera with a blue, mixed drink. She hated the picture but it fit her. He had a feeling he knew why she was calling so he answered immediately. "Hey, Zoe."

"Vincent proposed to Jordan!" she practically shrieked, her excitement for her brother clear.

Blue opened the refrigerator of the condo Red Stone had put him up in for this job and grabbed a beer as he said, "Not surprised."

She paused. "Did he tell you?"

"No, but come on, it's not a surprise to you either." Vincent had been in love with her for seven years and even though Blue had never heard of her until recently—none of them had—he'd seen the way they looked at each other.

"Okay, not really. Wish you could've been here to celebrate with us."

"Me too." Sort of. He was incredibly happy for his friend, but he'd needed to decompress more than he'd realized. The short job Harrison had put him on in Key West after that whole mess with Jordan's stalker had been welcomed instead of returning to his empty home in Miami. Adjusting to the civilian world was harder than Blue had imagined and being around a big crowd of people celebrating, drinking and laughing...it sometimes got to be too much. "Have you told your brother about your problem?" The one that Blue had come down here last week to help her out with. The one that *still* wasn't resolved.

"No, and I'm not going to. And neither are you. It's not an issue right now so...let's just forget about it."

"That's never going to happen," he said mildly, knowing that yelling rarely worked with Zoe. Even if he wanted to shout at her for being so stubborn. Opening the sliding door that led to the small patio, Blue inhaled the fresh, ocean air as he sat at the round, glass table. The sun was setting and most of the people at the pool below were gathering their things. It was one of the reasons he liked this place. With the pool area closed off after dark, it tended to stay quiet.

"I know, I just...I don't know what to do. There really isn't anything *to* do at this point. He's out of the country for six months." Relief punctuated her words.

"So what happens when he returns, Zoe?" Blue couldn't keep the edge out of his voice. He'd held off on telling Vincent about the man who had been basically stalking her only because she hadn't told Blue about it until he'd arrived in Key West a week ago. But by then the guy harassing her had left the country for work. And Blue had checked up to make certain.

"I'll worry about that then. Listen, I know I let it go on for longer than I should have but I was in a bad position." Her voice held a pleading note for him to understand.

If it was anyone else, Blue might have read them the riot act, but he couldn't with Zoe. She was smart and had been doing what she thought was best. "I don't like lying to your brother. Give it a couple days then tell him everything."

"I will, just not tonight."

"All right." He'd let it go for now. But if she didn't come clean soon he had to tell Vincent.

"Enough about that. What are you doing now that your job is over? Let me guess," she said before he could answer. "You're sitting alone in that condo drinking a beer and watching some game on TV."

"Wrong." But she was close enough that it made him uncomfortable.

"You're such a liar. You need to go out tonight and find a woman. Go out and have a good time. Stop living like an old man."

Closing his eyes, he leaned his head back against the cushioned chair and closed his eyes. "I don't want to find someone for a quick fuck." He'd had enough of those when he was younger. Now...hell, he didn't know what he wanted, but it wasn't that.

"Who says it has to be quick?" He could hear the laughter in her voice.

"Shut up. You know what I mean. I wish we were attracted to each other." It would make things a hell of a lot easier.

She made a mock gagging sound. "Eww."

"Seriously, you do wonders for my ego."

"Whatever. You are right though. If we were together it would get my mom off my back."

Blue grinned at that. "Yeah, she's a little terrifying."

"No kidding. Hey... speak of the devil, that's her," Zoe whispered. "I'm hiding in Vincent's bedroom so I've gotta go. But promise me you'll at least go out tonight. Not for a woman, but go out to eat somewhere. Just get out of that condo and see real people."

"Zoe—"

"Promise," she demanded.

"Fine."

"Next time I see you I'll know if you lied to me."

"I promise," he gritted out, knowing it was the only way he'd get her off the phone.

"Crap, I've really got to go now." She disconnected before he could respond.

Sipping on his beer, he stared out at the now empty poolside, hating that his friend was right. Zoe had a way of seeing right through his bullshit. It was why he considered her one of his best friends. Something he'd never thought he'd have from anyone else after leaving the Marines. The men he'd fought side by side with were his brothers, his best friends, but Vincent and Zoe had become family in the last year in a way he was incredibly grateful for. But it still didn't fill the void he felt growing inside himself a little every day. He just didn't...fit in here anymore. Too many things had happened; he'd changed too much.

Sighing, he set his half-empty beer on the table and stood. She was right. He needed to get the hell out of this condo, just for a couple hours.

* * *

Mina slipped the check Jerome Charron had just handed her into her purse. She was surprised and very grateful for the large amount. "Thanks for this."

He smiled in that charming way of his. "I should be thanking you. The tourists and even locals can't get enough of your work. I've seen a doubled increase in business compared to July last year. Part of it's from the busier cruise season, but part of it is your paintings. I'm going to start charging more. We'll both get bigger cuts and it will drive up the demand of your work—which is clearly worth it."

Though the thought of him increasing the price made her panic, she nodded. She hated the business aspect of her work even though it was necessary. And Jerome was very savvy when it came to making money. He'd recently put her in contact with the owner of The Playhouse, an exclusive club in Las Vegas, for commissioned work. That had been a welcome first. Normally she painted, then hoped her work sold. To be paid for work she hadn't even delivered was still a little surreal. And the bonus she'd received after delivery had been even better. "Whatever you think is best."

"That's what I like to hear, *ma chère*." At the sound of the bell over the front door ringing, he flicked a quick glance over her shoulder. "We're about to close in ten minutes but feel free to look around."

Mina half-turned to see a middle-aged, well-dressed couple entering the shop. Their skin was nicely bronzed with the slightest undercurrent of a reddish hue, as if they'd stayed in the sun just a little too long today. She guessed tourists. The husband nodded and the wife smiled as they strolled in, taking their time.

She turned back to her friend. "I know you've got to close up so I'll get out of your hair."

"You're never in my hair. And don't go, I'm meeting Lee for drinks in half an hour. You should join us. Maybe you'll meet someone."

Smiling politely, she took a small step back and shook her head. "I recognize that tone and no way." Lee was Jerome's life partner. They'd been together over thirty years and she adored them both. But every time they invited her to dinner, they always surprised her with a blind date. She wasn't falling for it again.

He held up his hands innocently. "No setups, I promise."

She snorted and headed for the door. "You are a terrible liar, but I'll see you later. I've got a couple new paintings to drop off next week if you've got the room."

"Bring them as soon as you can."

"I will." The bell jingled overhead as she left, though she barely noticed it when she stepped outside.

The blast of heat compared to the cool air-conditioning of the store was immediate. Considering she was from California where humidity was a much different, rarer beast than it was here, the Florida summers had taken some getting used to. This was her second one and sticky heat and all, she loved it. Smiling at one of the street vendors selling cheap plastic hurricane cups and other useless knickknacks, she ducked down a side street instead of heading straight along Duval to her condo. It was too late to deposit her check and the bank was closed over the weekend so she'd have to do it Monday. Tonight she planned to veg out, drink wine and relax. Tomorrow she might meet up with some friends for breakfast, but she needed to work. Okay, *wanted* to work. Getting lost in her paintings was usually when she was happiest.

After growing up in a house where being an artist was akin to being a terrorist, she'd embraced her new life and freedom as much as she could. If she wanted to spend the whole day working, she would and there was no one to make her feel guilty about it or act as if what she did was frivolous or flighty.

Glancing over her shoulder, she started to step off the curb to cross the street when a flash of movement caught her eye from the other side of the road. A man stepped out from behind a low hanging palm tree branch that fell over the wall from the other side. He appeared as if from nowhere and even though this alley was well-lit, it was as if he was intentionally sticking to the few shadows there. His movements were slow but purposeful, making her nervous.

Okay, more than nervous. Alarm bells were going off in her head. Before moving to Key West and actually since living here she'd been adamant about paying attention to her surroundings. But she'd gotten caught up in her head, not thinking about anything. Wondering if she was being paranoid, but not really caring, she picked up her pace and started jogging toward the end of other road. Her sandals—not designed for running—made loud snapping sounds each time she hit the pavement.

Nerves humming through her, she glanced over her shoulder again and nearly stumbled. No one was on the other side of the road. Frowning, she turned and started to pick up her pace again when a man jumped out from one of the cars parked along the curb.

When she saw the knife held loosely in his hand, she instinctively reacted. Screaming at the top of her lungs, she hauled her purse back and slung it at him. Surprise flitted across his features for a moment, giving her the element of surprise as he ducked back, but she only clipped his face. She swung her heavy bag again, aiming at his middle, but he grabbed it mid-air and yanked.

Though she hated to give him her purse, she let go. Everything in it was replaceable and not worth losing her life. Continuing to scream, she pivoted and dodged between two parked cars, trying to put distance between them. As her feet hit the cobblestone street, another man jumped up from behind one of the cars.

Another scream built in her throat, tearing free with bloodcurdling volume. She wasn't physically strong or stupid enough to think she could take on two men. But she could scream loud enough to bring help while she fought back. Or she hoped.

As she shouted for help, she dodged around the end of the car to the right, away from the other man. Unfortunately that put her right back in the path of the first one.

Panic, slick and icy slid down her spine as she came face to face with her first attacker. He wasn't holding her purse and the knife was gripped firmly in his hand.

His dark eyes seemed bottomless as he watched her with no expression. As if he was looking right through her.

She started to scream again when a hand clamped over her mouth. The stench of stale cigarettes filled her nostrils and mouth as she started to struggle.

The numbness that had threatened to take over her cracked free, only to be replaced by raw fear that this wasn't merely a robbery.

CHAPTER TWO

Mina threw her elbow back, ignoring the pain as she connected with the man's ribs. He grunted, but barely seemed affected. Another shot of raw fear slammed through her as his grip tightened. She started thrashing around and the man in front of her began to advance but suddenly froze, his eyes growing wide as he growled a curse. Then he raced past them and suddenly she was falling. Scrambling to hold on to something, anything to stabilize her, her fingers skimmed the near-by car before she fell onto the cobblestone road.

Despite the pain that ricocheted up her spine, she rolled over and pushed up, expecting to have to defend herself. Instead she saw one huge man fighting with three—three!—in the middle of the quiet road. He slammed his fist against the jaw of the man who'd covered her mouth. Even from this distance she could hear the crack. The man with the knife lunged at him but he kicked out at him like some sort of ninja, throwing her would-be attacker back a couple feet. Though it felt like forever, she knew only seconds had passed as they fought.

And she had to get help.

Scrambling back in between the cars toward the sidewalk, relief punched through her when she saw her purse near a wooden privacy fence that lined this side of the alley. Half of her belongings were strewn across the pavement, including her cell phone. Snagging it off the ground, she started to dial 9-1-1 when the sound of squealing tires made her head jerk up. A dark SUV with tinted windows was racing out the other end of the alley, thankfully in the opposite direction. But the big man who'd come to her rescue was lying on the ground.

Phone in hand she raced down the sidewalk, fighting panic that he'd been injured or worse. Maybe the guy with the knife had stabbed him... As she reached him, he groaned and shoved up to a sitting position.

"Are you okay?" he rasped out as he glanced around, diligently taking in their surroundings.

"I should be asking you that." Kneeling next to him, she reached out to touch his temple. "Thank you so much for what you did..." A small trickle of blood trailed down the side of his face. "Crap, you're bleeding."

"It's nothing," he muttered, swiping it clean, but didn't move away from her.

"Are you hurt anywhere else?" She scanned him, taking in the casual pants and loose T-shirt. That was when she saw the gun peeking out from underneath his shirt which had been shoved up. It was secured to the side of his pants by a small holster. Mina jerked to a halt at the sight of the weapon. Her throat constricted, but before she could move, he pushed up to a standing position and held out a hand for her.

"I have a permit and I'm fine, but we need to call the police. Whoever those guys were, they weren't just out to mug you. They shot me with a fucking bean bag round." He groaned as he pulled her to her feet.

At five feet eleven, she was taller than a lot of people so she was surprised when she stood in front of him and realized he had to be well over six feet. And he was really broad too. There couldn't be an inch of fat on the guy. And why was she noticing that anyway? Maybe she had hit her head. "Wait, what?" His words finally registered as she tore her gaze from his wide chest to his concerned face. "A bean bag? What are you talking about?" And why had he even jumped in to help her like that? She wanted to ask but was struggling to remain calm.

He nodded at the ground and stepped past her. She watched as he bent down and when he came back up with something in his hand she was even more confused at what she saw.

He held it up for her to inspect. "They shot this at me using a shotgun with some sort of modifier on it. I've never seen something like that before. I barely heard the release."

"You mean they shot you with something police use in riot controls?" That was beyond weird. But also deadly. She'd read an article about the kind of damage those things could do if they hit someone in the head or ribs. "Where did they hit you?"

"Barely clipped my shoulder. Trust me, I'm fine," he said as he scanned her from head to foot. "Did they hurt you? Did they say anything?"

A shiver raced through her as the reality of what could have happened slammed into her all at once. "They didn't hurt me, but they would have." As thoughts of how truly horrific tonight could have gone settled in her mind, another shiver took hold and soon she was full-on shaking, her teeth chattering even as she tried to speak. There had been three of them. She hadn't even seen the third until that fight. And there'd been a driver, so that was four.

"Shit," he muttered, pulling her into a tight embrace. The sudden hold should have shocked her but she was barely hanging on after what had just happened. "You're okay." A big, surprisingly gentle hand, soothingly stroked down her back, helping steady out her breathing and slow her heart rate.

Despite the fact that she was standing in the middle of the street—where the hell was anyone else?—with a stranger, she felt oddly safe in his arms. Still clutching her phone, she wrapped her arms around him and buried her face against his chest. He smelled fresh, like clean linen with just a hint of a spicy aftershave. She struggled to find her voice, but couldn't make her throat work as it tightened.

"Don't try to talk just yet," he murmured, slowly walking them until they reached the sidewalk. "Step up."

She did as he said then took a deep, shuddering breath as she stepped out of his embrace. "I'm okay. Sort of." Enough to talk anyway. "Again, thank you for saving me. If you hadn't been here..." Shuddering again, she trailed off. She so didn't need to say the words aloud. The images were already vivid enough in her crazy imagination. "Are you a cop or something?"

He shook his head before glancing around. "No, but we need to call them now. And get you out of this alley. I don't like how cut off it is from everything."

She wasn't going to argue with getting the hell out of there. "My purse," she blurted, nodding down the sidewalk where the contents of her bag were strewn about.

He fell into step beside her as they headed for it. "What's your name?"

"Mina. You?"

"Alexander, but you can call me Blue. It's my last name."

Despite the remnants of fear clinging to her insides like kudzu, she let out a short laugh. "Blue?"

He lifted those broad shoulders, still not looking at her as he scanned the alley. God, she wanted to punch herself for walking down here alone. The city was relatively safe and this was a great neighborhood, but seeing it through a stranger's eyes, she realized how truly quiet and cut off this street was. There weren't any shops on it so no one had any reason to be down here unless they were cutting through. Like she'd stupidly done. That's what she got for getting complacent. Back in California she'd never have done something like this.

Of course there she would never have been allowed anywhere without armed freaking guards. She raked a shaky hand through her hair as they reached her belongings. "Listen...I don't want to call the cops."

He pinned her with that dark gaze, making her squirm. The man was like a statue standing there. "Why not?"

She blinked, surprised he wasn't immediately insisting she do it. "It's complicated. Besides, what are they going to do except take a report? We'll have to go down to the police station and make a statement. Then what? Did you get the license plate?"

He shook his head. "There was mud rubbed on it. But I got a good look at all those guys. And so did you. Right?"

"Two of them." But if they went to the police it would eventually leak to the public who she was. Only a few people in Key West knew her real name and she trusted them implicitly. She'd been using her mother's maiden name since she moved here so she could live in peace with relative anonymity. It wasn't that her father was famous, just filthy stinking rich. And certain people would recognize her last name and try to capitalize on that. Or worse, hurt her. If she filed a report—and she couldn't give a fake last name to the cops—and the media got wind of it... Yeah, not happening. She wasn't going to sit back and just do nothing, but... "I'm not filing a report," she insisted before bending to gather her things.

He knelt next to her and started helping. She was surprised, but relieved he didn't argue. "This isn't a purse, it's like a fucking suitcase," he muttered.

She laughed at his analysis because it was true. He handed her a fallen e-reader, then a new pack of paint-brushes she'd bought on her way to Jerome's, as she gathered up everything else. When he paused, she frowned upon seeing what he'd picked up.

And felt her face heat.

He was holding two condoms. The silver wrapper with the word Playhouse in bold, black lettering was unmistakable. They looked so small in his big hands, which made a very feminine part of her tighten unex-pectedly. When she'd had the painting for the Playhouse delivered they'd not only paid her, but sent her a very creative gift basket with all sorts of toys. Some things she hadn't even known what they were used for until she'd Googled them. She'd planned to give the condoms and flavored lube to Jerome—thank God the lube hadn't fallen out of her purse—but had forgotten after seeing the amount on her check.

"Those aren't..." She cut herself off, not needing to explain anything to this stranger. She hadn't had sex since she moved to Florida, not that that was any of his business. If she wanted to walk around with an entire arsenal of condoms and sex toys it was no one's business but hers. Snatching them from his hand she shoved them into her purse. When she met his gaze again she was surprised by the flash of hunger in that dark gaze.

Unable to find her voice, she finally drank him in. All of him. Crouching there on the sidewalk he looked like a tiger, ready to pounce. Not necessarily on her, but there was a lot of strength and power in that body. That very muscular, very large body. And something told her that he was proportionate *everywhere*. With the sharp, de-fined lines of his face, he'd be a dream to paint. And sculpt. That thought made her hands itch to do just that. As her gaze landed on his lips she was struck by how soft they were in comparison to the rest of him. Soft, kissa-ble...

When he cleared his throat she felt her face heat up again as she met his gaze. And that hunger was still there. It was muted now, but definitely simmering be-neath the surface in those dark brown eyes. "Seriously, thank you for what you did. I can't believe you took on all those men for a stranger. Can I buy you dinner or something? Please." It was a lame way to thank him, but she couldn't think of anything else.

Sighing, he rubbed a big hand over his face. "You *should* call the cops," he muttered.

She ignored his words as she saw his bruised knuckles. "You're hurt," she said, sounding more accusing than she'd meant to.

Reaching out, she took his right hand in hers. It might have been her imagination but an electric current seemed to jolt through her at the contact. His palm and fingers were rough and callused as she inspected his knuckles. He jerked slightly at her touch, but didn't pull away.

"This is nothing," he muttered in that deep gravelly voice that did strange things to her insides.

Frowning, she shook her head and stood. "It's not *nothing.* You're coming back to my place so I can patch you up." When it seemed like he might argue, she continued. "It's not up for discussion." She couldn't explain it, even to herself, but she wanted to take care of this man after everything he'd done for her. Fighting off all those men, and for a stranger, it was incredible.

His dark eyes widened as he stood next to her—towering over her. Men never towered over her, never made her feel small and petite, but this guy did. It was jarring. Exciting. "Fine. But you're telling me more about those men," he said as they headed down the sidewalk.

"What's to tell? I don't know them." As music and the sounds of happy, drunk people reached her ears, a sense of calm slid through her.

"But you know why they wanted to take you." He wasn't asking. "Because those guys didn't have mugging or rape in mind." His blunt words made her stumble as they reached the end of the sidewalk. As if realizing what he'd said he cursed under his breath. "Sorry."

She shook her head, fighting off a shiver as she pointed left. "This way. And I really don't know what they wanted." But she had a small idea. Maybe. She needed to call her father as soon as she had some privacy. Then she would take action and hire security if necessary—which she was ninety-nine percent sure it would be. Involving the cops would be pointless and while she was very appreciative of this stranger's help she wasn't going to tell him everything. Especially not since he had a gun. The guy had saved her so she wasn't worried about him hurting her. Well that and her internal radar wasn't pinging out of control. She'd learned at a young age to figure out who was an asshole and who wasn't. Blue definitely wasn't.

"Hmm." The sound he made indicated he didn't believe her. But he didn't say anything else, just stayed close to her as they headed down the sidewalk. When they neared a cluster of drinking college-aged kids laughing and clogging up the sidewalk, he wrapped an arm around her shoulders and steered around them. "Stay close."

A delicious shiver raced down her spine as she slid an arm around his taut waist. It felt weird to snuggle up to a stranger but after what had just happened she didn't mind in the least. His warmth and strength were reassuring. Her nerves felt frayed the more she thought about what could have happened and all she wanted to do was get to the safety of her apartment.

He was silent as they walked, which was fine with her. When she was working on a project she would sometimes go for days without talking to anyone and this was a comfortable silence. But there was something she didn't understand about this Blue.

"Why are you helping me?" she finally asked as they crossed the second-to-last street before her building.

"Why wouldn't I?" he asked almost absently as he continued scanning, so vigilant she had to wonder at what kind of training he had.

Because this man was trained. She'd had her fair share of bodyguards over the years and had no doubt Blue had a similar background. In that moment, she wanted to know a lot more about this tall, sexy man who'd gone out of his way to help a complete stranger—

and didn't even want her to look at his injury, because he was more concerned about her.

CHAPTER THREE

Blue watched as Mina slid out a key card and put it into the slot on the silver pad next to the elevator. Tall, leggy, slender, with long dark hair that fell around her shoulders and breasts in soft waves, she was a fantasy come to life. When she looked up at him he realized she also needed to type in a code in the keypad next to it. Of course she wouldn't want him to see it. He turned away so she could do it with privacy.

He couldn't believe that she didn't want to call the police after what had happened. He could have pushed, but it wasn't his business. That didn't mean he was letting this go though. Not when she could still be in danger.

Those guys had been professionals. Not as trained as him and clearly stupid since they hadn't been wearing masks—or maybe they hadn't cared about her seeing their faces, which was even more concerning. Though the fact that they'd hit him with a bean bag gun instead of using real bullets had been surprising. And telling about some of their intent. He'd been busy grappling with two of them when another man from the interior of that SUV had pumped a round at him. It had taken him off guard but luckily they'd run instead of continuing to open fire. He hadn't wanted to use his weapon in a semi-public place unless absolutely necessary, though he would have done it without pause if they'd shot at him again.

Once they were in the interior of the small elevator, Mina's sweet tropical scent wrapped around him. He felt tongue-tied around her, and it was more than just his adjustment to the civilian world. He had no problem talking with female friends. But he didn't want to sleep with his friends. Mina, however, made his entire body come to life. And after finding those condoms in her purse, all he could think about was using them with her. Which wasn't like him. He hadn't been with a woman since he'd returned to the civilian world. Hell, he hadn't been with anyone during his last deployment either. Mainly because it was too fucking hard to give anyone that level of trust.

He still had occasional nightmares and didn't want anyone to see that. Especially not a woman. Of course he didn't have to stay the night with anyone, but he wasn't in to one-night stands. Not since his early twenties. Even though he was thirty-three, going on thirty-four, some days he felt like he was a hundred.

"What are you thinking about? You seem very deep in thought right now." Mina's soft voice broke him out of his thoughts.

Dragging his gaze back down to her, he found himself ensnared by her deep green eyes. They were like a forest green, so dark they almost appeared brown. And he could feel himself drowning in them. Tearing his gaze away wasn't any better. He drank in the sight of her like a starved man and she was the only thing that could quench him. God, what the hell was wrong with him? The ankle length dress she wore was thin and clung to her in all the right places, not hiding a single delectable curve. He didn't know much about women's fashion but he was pretty sure the style was called Bohemian. Whatever it was, it was fucking hot. Covered in a multicolored pattern of greens and browns the top of the dress was a halter style, with two rope-looking things that tied around the back of her neck. And right now all he could think about was pulling that tie free so he could find out what color her nipples were, because he was certain she wasn't wearing a bra. Scrubbing his hand over his face, he looked away. "Just wondering if you always invite strange men up to your place."

She stiffened next to him. "I don't, but even if I did it wouldn't be any of your damn business."

God, he was such a jackass. Realizing how that had sounded, he turned to her as the elevator stopped on the third floor. "I didn't mean it like that." He'd meant it from a security perspective. "I...I'm shit with people. I was thinking of something I shouldn't and didn't want to say it out loud. I'm sorry." What the fuck had gotten in to him? He couldn't believe the shit just rolling out of his mouth right now. He sounded like the biggest moron on the planet. Yeah, she was going to tell him to get the hell out of here right now. He stayed in the elevator, waiting for her to change her mind.

To his surprise, her green eyes lit up as she smiled and motioned to the open doors. "I'm shit with people too. Come on."

Pushing out a breath of relief he hadn't realized he'd been holding, he followed her out—and tried to ignore the soft sway of her ass as she headed for one of the two doors along the tiled hallway. She was slender and lean, but her curves were perfect. "This is me."

Shit, this place was more than just *nice*. The fairly non-descript pastel blue four-story building located on a side street right off Duval had to be prime real estate. The location was close to the water, in a safe area and quiet enough that he couldn't hear any music or other noises coming from the restaurants and clubs he knew were nearby.

"Wait," he demanded as she put her key in the door.

She glanced over her shoulder, her eyes wide. "What?"

"Do you have an alarm system?"

She nodded. "Of course. And it's always armed."

"Okay." Those men hadn't targeted her randomly, something he was fairly sure she was aware of. So it stood to reason that her own home might be a target. Yeah, he didn't like this one bit. He wanted to insist on going in first, but didn't want to push his luck.

Once inside the beeping of her alarm sounded. After she turned it off, she immediately re-armed it to stay mode, which eased some of his tension. Barely. He wanted to see how good this system was. "So, what do you do?" he asked as she headed down a short, tiled hallway, unable to help but notice the extra number of security sensors along the tops of the walls. That was good—and interesting.

"I'm an artist. I sell my paintings and occasionally sculptures through a couple local shops, but recently— very recently—I did my first commissioned job. I'm hoping it's not the last..." She trailed off as they reached the end of the hallway. Directly to their left was a small kitchen and that opened up into a living room and what he was certain was supposed to be a dining room area, but she'd turned it into a mini-library. It was filled with colorful paintings of ocean life and books, some on shelves and others stacked on the floor. It should appear cluttered, but it wasn't. It was bright and full of life. A stark difference to his own condo in Miami. "Sit in there, I'll be right back," she said, pointing to one of the couches in the living room. Without glancing at him she disappeared to the right down a short hallway to what he assumed was her bedroom.

He heard her talking to someone and wondered if someone else lived here, but by the brief conversation he realized she was on the phone. Or at least leaving a message.

Looking at his bruised knuckles, he made his way to the living room and did as she said. The furniture was simple and mostly a light brown, but she had colorful throw pillows, blankets and art dotting the room making it seem alive. Minutes later she returned with a first aid kit in her long, elegant fingers. Her care was unnecessary, but he wanted to feel her hands on him again so he didn't say anything.

She sat on the solid-looking wood coffee table in front of him and held out her hand. "So tell me about yourself, Blue," she said as she gently turned his hand over, inspecting the slight abrasions on his knuckles. "Are you in town for work or pleasure?"

"Both." One word was all he could manage with her touching him. He couldn't remember the last time a woman had touched him so gently.

At that, she looked up, eyebrows raised as she set his hand on his leg. "Want to expand a little?"

He cleared his throat. After leaving the military he'd gone straight to work for Red Stone Security and wasn't used to talking to anyone other than the men and women he worked with. Mainly about work stuff. The people they guarded didn't converse with them much and vice versa. Which was the way it had to be. He couldn't be doing his job if he was interacting with the clients. He was there to protect them, not be their friends. "I was here for work, then my boss told me to take a few days' downtime, so I am."

"What do you do for a living?" She opened the small kit and pulled out a foam disinfectant, leaning in close again.

Her scent taunted him, making his brain short-circuit like a teenager who'd never talked to a girl before. Except he'd never been an awkward kid. Back then girls had fallen into his lap. Just like in college. Things had been different after, but he didn't want to think about any of that now. He needed to answer her. When she took his hand in hers again, he fought to speak, much less think. It was damn hard when all he wanted was to feel her soft hands stroking every inch of him. "Personal security."

Her eyebrows pulled slightly together as she squeezed the disinfectant on his knuckles. "Like a body-guard?"

"Yeah, for the most part."

She paused but didn't comment. "Does this sting?" Concern filled her voice as she met his gaze again.

He fought a smile and shook his head. "It tickles."

She immediately relaxed and pulled out a tube of antibiotic cream.

"That's not—"

"Let me do this please." Her voice and hands shook slightly as she twisted the top off. "You literally fought off three men to save my life and I know this doesn't make up for it but I need to do something."

That was when he realized she was still upset. Not that he blamed her. Reaching out, he stilled her fingers with his own, forcing her to look at him. "How are you doing? It's still not too late to call the police."

"I know, I just...it's not the best thing for me. I'm not going to do nothing though, so don't worry about that. And I'm not sure how I'm doing. Freaked out pretty much sums it up." She shook her head before returning to her task.

When she smoothed the ointment on his knuckles he was struck by how gentle she was. She had little calluses on the pads of her fingers, likely from painting or sculpting. Nothing like the big ones he had. It jarred him how much he enjoyed the feel of her touching him, especially when he imagined what it would feel like to have her wrapping those fingers around a much lower part of his anatomy. Shit, he couldn't think of that. He was already half-hard just sitting there.

"Were you in the military?" Her sudden question threw him, but he nodded.

"Yeah. Marine Corps. Ten years. How'd you know?" Unlike a lot of Marines, he didn't have any tattoos.

"Just a guess. The way you took those men down made me think you had to have some kind of training and the military makes the most sense." She twisted the cap back on. "I can put a light bandage on but I don't think you need one."

He shook his head. "I'm good, but thanks." Staring into her eyes, he tried to think of something, anything, intelligent to say. He didn't want to leave just yet, but knew if he couldn't fucking talk like a normal human being there'd be no more reason to stay and she'd want him to leave. Rightly so.

"Are you hungry or thirsty?" She nervously smoothed her hands down her dress.

Unable to stop himself, he dragged his gaze down the length of her smooth, kissable neck all the way to the swell of—He shook himself and instead of looking into her eyes again, turned to the covered French doors. "Thirsty." An entire word, good for him. He wanted to kick his own ass.

"I think I've got wine and water. No beer though," she said as she stood, taking that sweet tropical scent with her.

It was a combination of vanilla, coconut and something that was all Mina. *Mina.* He wondered how her name would sound on his tongue. "Wine's good."

"Do you have any plans tonight or do you want to hang out?" There was an odd note in her voice that he couldn't read.

Standing, he followed her into the kitchen, watching as she pulled out a bottle of unopened white wine from the stainless steel refrigerator. "Are you nervous to be alone?"

Biting her bottom lip, she nodded. "I've called my...someone about this, but for now, yeah I'm scared. But I know I have no right to ask you to stay with me. It's not like I need a babysitter or anything. I've got a security system. Forget it, I'm being stupid. You don't have to feel obligated—"

"I don't." And he didn't want her to be alone. Even if she wouldn't call the police he wanted to do a little digging into this on his own. He simply couldn't walk away when he knew someone was in danger, let alone this sweet, gentle woman. The fact that she was impossibly sexy didn't play into his decision to stay at all. *Right.*

Her shoulders relaxed and a half-smile pulled at her full lips. "If you're sure you don't mind, I know something fun we can do."

At those words, all sorts of images flooded his mind, most of which involved them naked. Since he wasn't sure what she meant he struggled to contain the physical reaction she evoked.

CHAPTER FOUR

At the sudden flare of heat in his dark eyes Mina's grip tightened around the wine bottle. Everything about Blue was so primal, so...freaking *huge*. He seemed to take up her entire kitchen. "Get your mind out of the gutter, I'm talking about innocent fun," she said teasingly, even if the magnetic pull she felt for him was undeniable.

He blinked, suddenly looking unsure and she felt bad for teasing him. "I wasn't..."

"I'm messing with you. Not about the innocent part, because whatever you're thinking isn't what I'm suggesting. I'm almost positive." She stared at him, daring him to contradict her.

To her utter surprise, a light dusting of color brushed over his tanned cheeks. He cleared his throat. "Yeah, probably."

Though she really wanted to ask what was going on in that head of his, she didn't—because she kind of already knew. She was too raw and even though something deep down told her that if she had sex with Blue right now it would be intense, she wanted to get to know him first. The whole situation was a little strange.

It still blew her mind that he'd helped out a stranger so selflessly and she didn't think she could handle anything other than talking anyway. Even if she was fantasizing about feeling his muscular body wrapped around hers, holding her close... no, no, no.

Feeling neurotic for her conflicting thoughts she grabbed two glasses and handed them to him. A shiver rolled through her as their fingers brushed and she refused to meet his gaze. Instead she pulled a wine bottle opener out of a drawer. "This way," she said, motioning toward the hallway. "There's a balcony through here." She opened the door to what was meant to be the master bedroom, but she'd turned into her art studio instead.

"Wow," he breathed as they stepped inside.

Glancing over her shoulder she saw him staring at her most recent piece. Even though she didn't favor expressionism as a rule, this one was. It was slightly blurred and very minimalist, but there was no doubt what the figures on the black and white painting were doing. A woman was flat on her stomach, her arms stretched out over her head and a man was behind her, in between her legs, his hands on either side of her head as he pumped into her. Apparently all her sexual frustration was making its way onto the canvas lately because this was the fifth one she'd done with this faceless couple. In each work they were in different sexual poses in the throes of passion. She inwardly cringed. He probably thought she'd wanted to show this to him.

"I forgot that was uncovered," she muttered. Then before she could stop herself she asked, "What do you think?" Immediately she wanted to take the question back. She almost never asked people that because the truth was, she didn't care what most people thought. She loved what she did and the way art made a person feel was subjective. She didn't want him to feel obligated to say he liked it.

He didn't answer right away, but when he looked at her his expression was thoughtful. "I don't know much about art, but I like it. It's sexual without being in your face about it. You're very talented."

The ring of truth in his words was like a warm caress over her. She felt silly for blushing, but heat rushed to her cheeks nonetheless. "Thank you." After pushing back the sheer curtains covering the sliding glass doors, she motioned outside to the covered patio. "When I bought this place, I had this patio enclosed with reflective glass." The summers could be brutally sweltering and she already had enough natural light with the other two windows in the room so she'd wanted to make this her little haven.

"It's right on the main strip." He sounded impressed as he stepped out next to her.

"Yeah." The building was an odd L-shape and most of it was on a quiet side street, but the back of some of the bedrooms faced Duval, giving her a perfect view of the bustling activity of the place. And a lot of inspiration for paintings. "I like to people watch, but maybe it's not as much fun as whatever you were thinking about in the kitchen."

He surprised her again by laughing, the sound deep and uninhibited—and it went straight to her core. God, when he laughed like that his whole face turned from serious stone to soft and not exactly boyish, but...relaxed. It definitely looked good on him. "I'm game to people watch," he murmured, capturing her with that dark gaze again.

Heat pulsed between her legs and it took all her willpower to step back from him and not indulge in what she wanted.

* * *

Lewis stood on the curb across the street from Mina Hollingsworth's place, looking at his cell phone instead of directly up at her condo. The crew he'd been working with to kidnap her had fucked up big time. Though to be fair, no one had expected that mammoth guy to come out of nowhere like a fucking super hero.

And now it looked as if the guy was still at her place. It was close to midnight and from what Lewis could see, the guy hadn't left. After their attempted kidnapping, the man they'd had sitting on her place had informed the crew that Mina had returned with the big guy shortly after their attack. Which made him wonder if she'd called the police at all. Her condo was too secured to attempt a breach and even though she didn't have many neighbors, they all had impressive security systems and many of them were retirees, home more often than not. So even if by some miracle they breached without setting off Mina's alarm, they wouldn't make it far without someone seeing or hearing them. Plus there were too many CCTVs in this area. It was why they'd decided to take her when she'd made a shortcut down that fucking alley. Everything had been perfect.

Until that big bastard showed up.

Putting his phone to his ear, he swayed slightly, faking that he was drunk as a couple holding hands walked past him on the sidewalk.

His contact picked up on the second ring. "Yeah?"

"She's home and still with that guy."

"He's at her place this late?" His voice was incredulous, but there was also a thread of unmistakable annoyance.

Lewis rolled his eyes. That's what he'd said. "Yeah."

"And none of you saw him around her these past few weeks?"

Lewis gritted his teeth. The woman didn't have a clockwork-like schedule so it had been more difficult to track her, but they'd done it well. He didn't like explaining himself but knew if he wanted to get paid he'd have to feign civility. "Nope. Had a few lunches with girlfriends but she spends most of her time painting or with Jerome Charron."

"Did you get a picture of the guy who saved her?"

"No. Happened way too fast. He was armed, though he didn't get a chance to draw his weapon." Lewis had no doubt the man would have though, if things had escalated any more. But his crew didn't use loaded guns with kidnapping jobs. Bean bag rounds, sure. But not anything with actual bullets. Too much room for error in his experience. Damaged or dead cargo was useless. And since he was the one running this team, he made the final decision about how the op went down.

"You should have killed him," the man snapped.

Lewis's lips pulled into a thin line. "And have a dead body left behind as evidence? Too messy. Look, she didn't call the cops. Or I don't think she did. This job is still a go. We just have to sit on her a little longer, look for a new angle." They hadn't been monitoring her calls because that was too time-consuming and too risky. Besides, there hadn't seemed to be a need when the man who'd hired them had given them a detailed file on her.

"You've got two days. Complete the job or you don't get the rest of your money." He disconnected before Lewis could respond.

Resisting the urge to glance up at the dimly lit balcony on Mina's floor, he shoved his phone in his pocket and began stumbling down the sidewalk until he was out of the line of sight before resuming his normal stride.

Taking the woman would be difficult because of her random schedule and because she was normally surrounded by people. Not only that, but this new man posed a threat. He was an unknown, a new piece to this puzzle and Lewis didn't like it because it was clear the guy had training. He'd moved in like a fucking killer and Lewis had seen the man's gun even if he hadn't used it. It was the only reason the crew had sped away. After missing a direct chest shot with the first bean bag shot, Lewis had known they wouldn't get a second chance without getting fired on. Part of him wondered if they should call it a day and walk from this job, but he'd come up against worse odds than one man before.

And the money he and his crew could get from taking the rich artist was too sweet a deal to pass up. They'd just have to get creative with how they took her.

CHAPTER FIVE

"I can't believe you actually played pro football. That's insane. I mean, I don't watch sports games, but it's still impressive." Stretched out on the cushioned lounge chair next to him, Mina was turned toward him, her long dress twined around her calves, wine glass in hand and a soft smile on her face.

Blue laughed again, something he'd been doing a lot of the past couple hours. Being around Mina was easy. He found himself opening up to her in a way he hadn't been comfortable doing in a long time. Sure he could blame it on the wine but he'd only had a couple glasses. "It's just sports, you don't have to say games. And it was only a year."

Her full lips pulled upward. "See? Shows you how much I know. What I do know, however, is that professional athletes tend to do pretty well for themselves. And you just left it all to join the Marines. I think it's incredibly honorable. And I don't mean this question offensively, but *why* would you leave like that?"

He took another sip of his wine before setting it on the small multi-colored wood table between them. Mina told him she'd refurbished and repainted it herself from some abandoned crates. "The short answer is 9/11 happened. I couldn't just live my life after that like nothing had happened." And his brother had died at the Pentagon that day. It didn't matter that more than a decade had passed, even thinking about it made his throat tighten in pain.

Her eyes widened slightly as she pushed up from her stretched out position. "That's...I don't even know what to say to that." She was silent for a long moment, watching him with those big eyes as if she could see right through him. "Was there more to it than that?"

He started to say no. It was more or less his default answer when anyone asked him anything personal. He glanced at his glass of wine trying to find the words. The pale liquid twinkled under the soft patio lights.

"Forget I asked. I didn't mean to pry." There was a panicked, apologetic note to her voice.

Fuck it. Even if he never saw Mina again after this night—though that thought was beyond depressing—he wanted to tell her this. Wanted her to know something real about him. "My older brother was at the Pentagon that day." Damn it. His throat closed up again, but he forced himself to continue. "So many people talk about where they were that day and I..." He rubbed a hand over his face, feeling shame for the shallow life he'd lived before. "I woke up with two women whose names and faces I can't remember. When I saw the news I was frantic to find out anything. Then when I did find out, I didn't want to know. Didn't want to believe that my brother was dead. After that..." He shrugged even though he felt anything but casual.

"After that you followed in his footsteps?" She was way too perceptive.

"Yeah. Went to OCS—Officer Candidate School—and was in for ten years." He'd been a poster boy for a while because of his brother's record and his own pro-athlete status, something that had been good and bad. Officers often had to prove themselves with their men because the enlisted men and women under their command had usually seen a hell of a lot more combat than them. It had been no different for Blue. He'd had to prove himself at first—rightly so—and all that acclaim from having played pro ball had just been a fucking albatross around his neck for the first year.

"That's incredible." Her voice was soft as she watched him.

Damn, he could drown in her dark green eyes. But he didn't want to talk about himself anymore. The topic was too fucking heavy for the night. And he wanted to know more about what kind of danger she was in. "Turnabout's fair play. I told you something I never tell people. Now you tell me why those men were after you. Because I know you know."

Cheeks flushing, she glanced down at her empty glass. "I think someone drank all my wine."

He snorted and she met his gaze again.

"Fine, you're right. I can't know for sure, but I'm pretty positive those men tonight targeted me because of my father. Warren Hollingsworth."

Blue shook his head, not recognizing the name.

Mina half-smiled. "I doubt you'd know his name. Most people don't. It's mainly known in scientific circles. He's incredibly wealthy and very paranoid, which is part of the reason I've distanced myself from him in the past couple years."

"What does he do?"

"Now he mainly funds projects not deemed worthy of further research because even if a cure is discovered, the financial payoff isn't worth it." There was a note of pride in her voice, so clearly she respected her father.

Blue nodded. "Because the pool of people affected by whatever the disease they're trying to cure is too small for big business to give a shit?"

A ghost of a smile played across her lips. "Exactly."

"You said 'now', so did he always just fund projects?"

She shook her head and for a moment he couldn't tell if she was going to continue. She idly played with the stem of her wine glass for a long moment. "No. He's truly brilliant and has discovered multiple cures for what we'd consider modern diseases. And while his name would mean nothing to the public, to pharmaceutical companies and the government, he's made of solid gold. He still tinkers, as he likes to call it, in his lab, but these days he likes to back underfunded projects and play with investments. I swear whatever he touches profits. He just has a gift for making money."

Blue knew he should be focusing solely on the threat still out there, but he wanted to know more about Mina. Wanted to know what made this sensual woman tick. "You two are close?"

She laughed, the harsh, bitter sound emanating from her a stark difference to the laid back woman he'd gotten to know in the last few hours. "I'm his greatest disappointment." At that, she looked away, staring out onto the street below. There were no tears, but a resigned sadness emanated from her and he wanted to take back his question.

It was late—or early, depending on how you looked at it—and only one or two people strolled by every few minutes as the bars were starting to close down. "I can't imagine you being a disappointment to anyone."

Her gaze snapped to his, narrowing as she watched him, as if she was gauging his sincerity. Then she shrugged, the action jerky. "Yeah, well...anyway, short answer to your question, I'm pretty sure I've been targeted because of his wealth. It wouldn't be the first time. I've already called his head of security and left a message apprising him of the situation." She glanced at her cell phone sitting on the small table. It hadn't buzzed or rang since they'd been out on the patio. "I'm surprised he hasn't called me back, but it went straight to voicemail so they might be on a plane. I'll try again in the morning."

"So why no police?"

"They can't do anything except maybe place a guard on my building. But if I fill out a report, all my personal information will eventually become public. Trust me, it's happened before. I've tried so hard to make a normal life for myself here and until I hear back from Ivan—that's my father's right hand man—I'm not involving the cops. I have a state of the art security system, a gun and...a panic room."

Blue's eyebrows raised. "Seriously?"

She nodded. "Yeah. It's small and not something I'd want to stay in long term, but if the alarm goes off, it's good enough to stay in until the police arrive. Seriously, I'm not oblivious to the potential danger, I just know that filling out a silly report will do nothing to protect me. When I moved here I wasn't stupid enough to shun my father's money. I used it to buy a safe, secure place so I could paint. Just because I'd put distance between us didn't mean would-be criminals would care and that I'd suddenly not be a target anymore. I've been using my mother's maiden name and living a very low key life." He could hear the desperation lacing her words.

She didn't want to give up her life and he couldn't blame her. He was also pretty certain she'd been targeted before from her tone. Whether stalked or actually kidnapped he couldn't be sure unless he asked. He would, but later. Right now he'd pushed too hard and the knowledge wouldn't affect his ability to protect her so he held off on asking.

Blue scrubbed a hand over his face and glanced out at the street again with a critical eye. He'd been scanning people coming and going all night with more than just Mina's people-watching curiosity. So far no one had stood out above the rest as potential threats. "I'd like to stay the night," he said bluntly, turning back to face her.

Her eyes widened for a moment. Then she shook her head, as if to clear it. "You mean, to protect me?" she asked, frowning.

He nodded even though he wanted to do a hell of a lot more than simply protect her. "I don't like this situation."

She didn't contemplate it long before she nodded. "I should probably tell you no. This isn't your problem, but...I'd feel safer with you here. You can have my bed and I'll sleep on the couch."

He was shaking his head before she'd finished. "I'll stay on the couch."

She just made a 'hmm' sound in her throat as she stood, as if she wasn't going to let that happen. Mina was a little bossy and oddly enough, he kinda liked it. He knew that would never extend to the bedroom—he just wasn't wired that way—but he loved her attitude. "I'm going to grab another bottle. Unless you're tired now?"

He wondered if she was intentionally changing the subject, but he shook his head and stood. "I'm good, but I'll grab it. You sit." The urge to take care of her even in a small way was so great it stunned him.

"Blue—"

"Call me Alex, or Alexander." He wasn't sure where the words came from, but suddenly he wanted to hear his given name on her lips.

"Okay, Alex." She stood there almost nervously and when her tongue darted out to moisten her lips, he got hard. Just like that.

He'd been struggling all night to keep his growing need for her at bay, to shove it ruthlessly back down. Most of the time it had worked because he'd been so caught up in conversation with her, but now in this stillness, with just the two of them...fuck. When she took a step forward, as if to close the small distance between them, his entire body tightened in need, his cock pressing against the zipper of his pants. But just as suddenly she sat back on the lounge chair.

Glancing down at her clasped hands, her dark eyelashes fanned her flushed cheeks. "Thanks for getting the wine," she murmured.

Fighting the disappointment that punched through him, he headed through the sliding glass doors to get another bottle of wine even though he'd rather be kissing every inch of her sweet body. He should have just fucking kissed her. It was clear she wanted him.

But Mina was different than the women he'd been with in the past. Back in college and his short pro ball days, women had wanted him for the status he could give them. And he'd been absolutely fine with that. Then in the Marines sex had been purely about release, about relieving the tension and stress during combat. He'd never even thought about anything long term with a woman and had purposely searched out women on the same page as him.

Mina...she was special. She was the kind of woman he could see something real with. And that scared the shit out of him.

* * *

Mina stretched out on her king-size bed, staring at the ceiling. After a couple more hours of talking, she and Alex had both decided to crash at four in the morning. The only time she ever stayed up that late was when she was painting and couldn't tear herself away. Even when she went out with friends she was usually home by midnight.

But she hadn't wanted to stop talking to Alex. Finally her body had won out though and she'd been forced to admit how exhausted she was. After showering and changing into pajamas—which she'd worn only because he was in her home—now she was wired again. Okay, maybe not wired so much as turned on and unable to sleep.

In the shower she'd tried not to fantasize about Alex. There had been such a vulnerability to him when he'd asked her to call him by his first name, as if he'd surprised himself. The more she'd tried to not think about him, all she'd been able to envision was him pinning her against the slick, tiled wall. Him taking her on the soft rug in her bathroom. On the hardwood floor of her bedroom. Or bent over the end of her bed... Clearly she was beyond sexually frustrated and Alex's presence was only exacerbating it. When he looked at her she knew he wasn't seeing dollar signs. No, he just saw her as a woman. A very desirable one.

The past few months she'd been edgy and needy and while she knew what the issue was she hadn't met a man she'd wanted to get naked with. She'd always had to be careful about who she got involved with in case they were targeting her for her family's money. Here she hadn't been worried much about that, but most of her friends were either women or gay men and the setups her friends had tried had all been wrong. Usually because they'd been artists and she didn't want to date a male version of herself.

Now an incredibly sexy, sweet and impossibly masculine man was sleeping on her couch and all she wanted to do was invite him to her bed. It was certainly big enough for the two of them.

Since she didn't think she was brave enough to march out there and ask him to join her, she slid her hand underneath the front of her light cotton pants until her middle finger slid over her pulsing clit. She hadn't bothered with panties, maybe because she'd known this was inevitable. Hell, why was she even fighting it?

As she imagined what it would look like to have Alex crouched between her spread thighs, his face hovering over her pussy, she began stroking her clit. She didn't even need to bother with her vibrator or any penetration. Just imagining what it would be like as Alex kissed her from head to foot, as he stroked his hands and mouth all over her body was enough to make her soaked for him.

Barely minutes later she was coming against her hand, not surprised by how fast her orgasm hit. It wasn't nearly as intense as it would have been with Alex pumping inside her, but it took the edge off. Rolling to the side as her pleasure surged through her, she buried her face against one of her pillows and let out an uncontrollable groan. As she came down from her high, a soft knock against her door had her guiltily yanking her hand from her pants.

"Mina, everything okay?" Alex asked quietly.

"Fine." Crap, why did her voice have to sound all high-pitched and guilty?

"I'm out here if you need me." His deep voice rolled over her, making her nipples tighten even harder.

"Okay, thanks." Though she wanted to tell him that she *did* need him in her room, she couldn't find the words to ask him in. She'd seen the hunger in his eyes but he could still reject her. And waking up to him tomorrow if he did turn her down—no way she could deal with that. She was such a coward.

Instead of being brave, she grabbed her pillow and shoved it over her face so he wouldn't hear her groan, this one a mix of frustration and self-disgust.

CHAPTER SIX

Blue leaned against Mina's countertop, watching the sausage in the frying pan sizzle as he talked into his cell phone. He'd already made a few phone calls this morning, trying to get them in before Mina woke up. "You sure you don't mind?" he asked his friend Carter, the last call he should need to make until after he'd talked to Mina about his plans to keep her safe.

The other man just grunted. "Don't even ask that... So is this Mina as hot as Zoe?"

Blue gritted his teeth at the question even though he knew his friend meant nothing offensive by it. Last week when he'd had to leave Zoe to help her brother and the Red Stone team out by watching Jordan during an op, he'd left Carter guarding Zoe. And the man hadn't been able to stop talking about how hot she was ever since. "Mina's off limits," he growled.

There was a short pause. "So this is more than work?"

"It has nothing to do with work."

"Oh. Shit. All right then. Yeah, just come by when you can and we'll get you guys set up. One of us will scope out the place, see if anyone turns up. Just text me the address and I'll head over in the next hour." Chris was Carter's brother and even though they worked well together the two men couldn't be any more different. Carter was a player whereas Blue wondered if Chris even dated.

"Thanks, I owe you." As he set his phone on the counter, he heard faint movement coming from the hallway.

A moment later Mina stepped into the kitchen, looking bleary-eyed, rumpled and good enough to eat. Her dark hair hung loosely around her shoulders and the green fitted T-shirt she wore let him know she wasn't wearing a bra. As her nipples started to get hard, he forced his gaze from her breasts to her face and found her staring at his bare chest.

Instinctively he patted his flat stomach and inwardly smiled when her gaze darkened and raked over his chest and abs. "I took my shirt off to sleep but I can put it back on—"

"No," she quickly cut him off then cleared her throat as if embarrassed. "I mean, do whatever makes you comfortable," she muttered before ducking her head and heading for the full pot of coffee on the opposite counter.

He liked that he had an effect on her because she sure as hell had one on him. She was all he'd been able to think about last night. He'd finally drifted off with thoughts of her naked and writhing underneath him only to wake up with an uncomfortable hard-on. He'd had to think of shitty things to finally get it to go away.

"You didn't have to cook," she said as she pulled a mug down from one of the cabinets and poured herself coffee. The woman had so many different flavors to choose from so he'd gone with the breakfast blend.

He shrugged. "I wanted to. Did you hear back from your father or his security?"

Leaning against the counter, mug in hand, she frowned as she shook her head. "No and that's not like either of them. I called my father this morning and it went straight to voicemail too."

"I hope you don't mind, but I made some calls to a few contacts about your situation." With the brazen attack still fresh in his mind, he hadn't been able to sit back and do nothing. Even if Mina kicked him out of her life, he'd had to involve others. Too much time was passing since the attempted kidnapping and he didn't want to lose any leads.

At his words, she straightened against the counter and set her mug down. He could see the flare of hurt in her gaze, but he shook his head before she could speak.

"*Not* to the police. People I work with and a couple guys I served with who live down here. What happened isn't going to be made public and the cops aren't going to be involved as of yet."

The tension in her shoulders lessened some as she leaned back again. "Okay. So who exactly did you talk to and what did you tell them?"

"I let my boss know everything about the attack. Red Stone has a lot of resources for this kind of thing." In addition to private security they also had a small branch dedicated to hostage negotiation when wealthy individuals didn't want to involve the authorities. Their success rate was almost perfect.

"One of the Caldwell brothers?" she asked, sipping her coffee, her eyes more alert now that she was waking up.

He nodded. Last night they'd talked about his job and she'd known enough about Red Stone Security that it surprised him. It didn't now that he understood her father had used Red Stone in the past. "Harrison. I told him who you are, what happened and the sensitive nature of the situation. No details of you and the life you've built here will be leaked to anyone."

"Why didn't you just wait until I woke up to ask me?" That hurt flickered in her gaze again, like a punch to his gut.

Blue turned the stove off and moved the pan to the side before turning to face her fully. "We went to bed late and I wasn't sure when you'd wake up. I wanted to get everyone in the loop as early as possible." And he hadn't been sure if she'd even say yes. He'd figured he could just do it then ask for forgiveness later.

She rubbed a hand over her face and slightly shook her head. "Okay, so what did your boss say?"

"They're looking into high profile kidnappings from the past year that fit a similar MO and one of Red Stone's security specialists will be looking at CCTVs in the city to see if they can dig up anything from around the time of the attempted kidnapping."

"That's smart... But why are they doing this? I haven't hired them or anything." She frowned, eyeing him warily.

Blue had figured this question would come and went for total honesty. "I can't be positive, but Harrison is a businessman. I think he's hoping that by helping you it will secure more contracts from your father. As soon as I told him your last name he was all over this."

A ghost of a smile tugged at her lips. Even if she didn't hire Red Stone, she'd pay them for services rendered. "At least you're honest." She took another sip and he let her digest everything before moving on. After a moment she spoke again. "I'd thought Ivan would have called me back by now with instructions on how to proceed but he hasn't. With Red Stone involved...what do I do now?" she asked and he could see the tension returning to her shoulders.

"Until and unless Red Stone is officially hired they're not getting overtly involved for legal reasons, though they'll continue to work in the background gathering information. But if you're willing, I'd like to stay with you in an unofficial capacity until your father's security contacts you or until you make a decision about your security. And I don't care if you hire a company other than Red Stone, until whoever came after you is found, you *need* protection."

Her eyes narrowed a fraction as she watched him. "And you're just doing this out of the goodness of your heart?"

Blue wasn't sure how to read her tone. "If I walked away and something happened to you I'd never forgive myself." He'd lost too many friends and even though he hadn't known Mina long, he wasn't walking away from this situation. From her. Even if she kicked him out, he was still watching out for her until this threat was eliminated.

Her expression softened immediately. "Sorry, I'm just so used to questioning motives of people. I know you're not like that. After a night of sleep I know I can't just sit and wait around anymore. I think I was just hoping I'd wake up and yesterday would be a bad dream."

Blue started to respond but she continued, surprising him. "Um, if I hire Red Stone can I request you as my personal security?" Her cheeks tinged pink as she asked.

Unsure what the protocol was and not particularly caring because he *would* be the one protecting her, he nodded. "I'm pretty sure you can request anything you want and get it." Red Stone's top priority was the safety and security of their clients and unless a client's request put them in danger, they went out of their way to keep people happy. Considering his attraction to Mina he should probably step back if she did hire Red Stone though.

But he was only human and that wasn't happening.

"You don't have to make a decision now. Eat, drink and finish waking up," he said softly.

She nodded and that dark green gaze tracked over his chest again, dipping low until she full-on blushed. Seeming to realize what she was doing, she glanced away and turned toward one of the cabinets. "Everything smells good. I don't even know what I have in my fridge so I can't imagine what you made."

Blue watched her lift up on her toes, grabbing plates. Her shirt pulled up, revealing a few inches of bare, tan skin and her skin-tight yoga-style pants molded to her perfect ass and long legs. His mouth watered at the sight. What he wouldn't give to taste every single inch of her delectable body. Feeling like a teenager with a crush, he turned around and started pulling the tortillas out of the plastic wrapping. "It's simple, but you had enough eggs and sausage for breakfast wraps."

She made an adorable snorting sound. "Usually I just go for coffee, but I could get used to this."

Something foreign and long-buried stirred deep inside him. Yeah, he could enjoy this on a regular basis too. He wasn't used to company in the morning—or ever. But he liked being around her, liked taking care of her... But that wasn't something he could dwell on. As he started cutting up the sausage, he said, "In addition to Harrison, I also contacted a couple friends of mine who live here. Carter and Chris Foley. They run a dive shop. Both former military." Carter had been in the Marines like Blue and Chris had been Delta. "If you're okay with it, Carter is going to sit on your place today and I'd like to get you away from here for a few hours." He looked over his shoulder to see her reaction.

Two plates in hand, she nodded. "I'd planned to paint all day, but I can take some time off. What do you have in mind?"

"Carter's going to let us use one of his boats. We can spend some time on the water away from any threat. He said there's a shallow reef near where he lives we can explore if you want. If we work it right, no one will even know we've left your place." Which would work best for their plan to keep an eye on her condo during the day. He didn't even want to bring Mina back here, but he didn't think she'd agree to up and leaving, however temporarily.

When she nodded, a mix of relief and hunger warred inside him. He wanted her away from here, but the thought of seeing her in a bathing suit was wreaking havoc on his senses. Right now he was walking a fine line. She hadn't officially hired Red Stone but if she did he couldn't be involved with her during any operations. Or...he shouldn't be.

* * *

Lewis sipped his iced latte as he slowly strode down the Hollingsworth woman's street. He had earbuds in his ears but his mp3 player was turned off. He just wanted to give the appearance that he wasn't paying attention to anything. The straw hat he wore was pulled low on his forehead. Combined with his sunglasses, it was enough to cover most of his face on the off chance the woman saw him. His attire was typical for tourists and locals so he wasn't worried about standing out from anyone else.

He and two other members from his crew were alternating shifts today watching her place. After losing her yesterday and the new two-day time frame in which to grab her, they had to sit on her condo in case she moved.

Unfortunately he wasn't certain they were the only ones watching her. Stopping on the sidewalk, he reached out and held onto a street meter, holding it for support while he bent down and pretended to pull a rock out of his sandal. Scanning the street, he saw the same truck he'd spotted earlier still parked in Mina's designated curbside spot. With these expensive condo complexes they had two parking spots; one in the interior parking garage and one right out in the open parking area in front of the building. There were only six spots in the small space in front of the building and hers was never in use since she used the interior garage only.

Now her exterior spot was filled and he could clearly see the familiar green tag given to residents hanging from the rearview mirror of the truck. Which meant she'd given her spot to that big guy from last night, or someone else. Someone who was likely staying with her. Security maybe. She was certainly rich enough to afford it.

That truck hadn't been there even two hours ago so this was a new development. Which just posed more questions. After covertly taking a picture of the license plate with his cell phone, he kept his stride casual as he headed in the opposite direction he'd come. He made his way into a quiet neighborhood and without glancing around, slid into the passenger seat of the waiting non-descript four-door car.

"You see anything?" Harry asked. He was the first man Lewis had brought in for this job. He was good with cracking safes and driving getaway cars. For this job, the latter was his primary function.

"Possibly. There's a truck sitting in her spot."

"Belong to the guy she's with?" Harry turned left on the next street, moving seamlessly into the flow of traffic.

"No clue. If it is, it means he left her to get it."

"Or he's brought in backup." His partner flicked a glance in the rearview mirror.

The plate had been local, not only to Florida but to Key West. Which meant the owner lived here. Lewis frowned as he went over the possibilities, then shook his head. The "what if" scenarios didn't matter. He pulled out one of his burner phones and texted another member of their crew to run the license plate using one of his contacts at the DMV. They'd find out soon enough who the vehicle belonged to.

Then they could take appropriate action against the owner if necessary.

CHAPTER SEVEN

Blue stood behind Mina on the dock as Carter held out a hand for her, helping her into the sleek, forty-foot Hatteras. This was Carter and Chris's personal boat, not one they used at their shop. It meant a lot that they were letting him and Mina use it. But their kindness did nothing to quench the surge of possessiveness he felt at seeing Carter grip Mina's hand.

The contact lingered a little too long as he helped her step onto the flat back of the boat. More likely that was Blue's imagination but ever since Carter had picked them up from her private garage, Blue had been feeling oddly possessive. He knew it was total fucking caveman stuff, but he wanted Mina all to himself.

Carter had that all-American, Hollywood handsome thing going on that even Blue could appreciate. The blond-haired blue-eyed man was also easy going and never wanting for female company. Something Blue was reminded of now as Mina smiled sweetly at something Carter said.

Stepping onto the boat behind her, Blue automatically scanned the open water for possible danger, but they were at the Foley brothers' house and he was ninety-nine percent sure no one had followed them. They'd been careful, getting into the backseat of Carter's SUV when he picked them up, and laying on the floorboards as they'd left. Having Mina stretched out on top of him like that, all those long, lithe curves pressed to his body had been heaven and hell.

Blue tried to shove the thought away so he wouldn't get another hard-on. Now was not the time to think about the short summer dress she was wearing. Or the visible thin straps of the black bikini tied around the back of her neck. All he'd been able to think about was what she would look like wearing just that two-piece suit. Hiding his erection from her had been impossible. She'd pretended not to notice but her face had flushed before she'd laid her head on his chest.

"Your place is beautiful, I didn't even realize this neighborhood existed," Mina said to Carter as she glanced over at their neighbors' docks. Six stretched out next to them, all sporting similar sized boats.

"Yeah, it's our little slice of paradise," Carter said, clearly proud and Blue didn't blame him. He knew what real estate went for in Miami and could only guess what this place was worth. Which told him that the Foley brothers were doing well for themselves.

"Will I get to meet your brother?" Mina asked, much more at ease than she had been when they'd made their covert escape from her condo.

"If you two join us for dinner tonight you will." Carter looked at Blue, eyebrows raised.

Blue hadn't discussed anything with Mina past this water excursion. She hadn't said one way or another whether she wanted to hire Red Stone and he hadn't pushed. Carter had stopped by Blue's place to grab a bag of clothes for him before picking them up. Then they'd come straight here. Blue didn't want Mina going back to her place at all, at least for the time being, but he wasn't sure how to bring it up. He was still getting to know her and he wanted to tread carefully with this situation so it didn't seem like he was taking over everything.

Before Blue could answer, Carter continued. "Y'all should just stay here anyway, at least for the night. With the threat right now, going back there isn't safe."

Swiveling from his friend, Mina pushed her sunglasses back on her head and eyed Blue questioningly. "Is that what you think we should do?"

Okay, she wasn't completely shooting the idea down. That was good. "It doesn't have to be here, but until you hire full time security and until we get a handle on who wants to kidnap you, it would be smart to put some distance between you and your place. I know it's secure but if they get desperate enough they might attempt to breach your condo anyway." Even if they failed in taking her, there was always a chance she'd get hurt.

She bit her bottom lip and nodded slowly. "I was hoping I'd have heard back from my dad by now, but..." She sighed. "Yeah, okay, I'll need more of my stuff, but that's definitely smarter. I just hate that someone is driving me from my home."

Carter clapped Blue on the shoulder as he stepped toward the back of the boat. "Just have Blue text us what you need and my brother will pack you a bag. If you want to stay here you're more than welcome. We've got two extra rooms."

Mina looked uncomfortable at that, probably because she didn't want anyone going through her belongings, or maybe because she didn't want to give her security code out, but she nodded. "Okay."

"I know you're armed, but there's extra hardware down below. Check under the pop up bench in the stateroom," Carter murmured only loud enough for Blue to hear before jumping onto the dock and beginning the process of untying the boat for them.

Blue had come more than prepared but was relieved to hear he had backup weapons if necessary. Not surprising considering the Foley brothers' military record.

As soon as Carter was out of earshot, Blue looked at Mina. "We don't have to stay here."

"No, you guys are right. And...I officially want to hire Red Stone. I keep expecting my dad to call, but this is on me. I've got to take charge of this. I just don't know how to go about hiring them. Should I call directly or..." She looked so lost as she stared at him and all he wanted to do was pull her into his arms.

"If you want to hire Red Stone then you can go back to your place tonight. We can still have dinner with Carter and Chris, but we'll meet the team this evening. Nothing has to change for your work schedule." Which he knew was important to her. "I'll talk to Harrison and set it up. I think you should start with a team of six. What do you think?" When she blinked at him, looking like a deer caught in headlights, he shook his head. "We'll start with six, but they should get a bead on these guys soon." He had absolute faith in the computer specialists and it wasn't like the men who had attempted to kidnap her were stalkers. A stalker was an entirely different beast whereas paid kidnappers usually wouldn't risk their lives if a job went south. They would just pull out.

"Okay." She stood there for a brief moment, watching him with an expression he couldn't begin to read. Taking him completely by surprise she wrapped her arms around him, pulling him into a tight hug. "Thank you for all you're doing. I'm embarrassed that I don't know how to handle all this stuff."

Savoring the feel of her lean body against his once again, he wrapped his arms tight around her. If Carter wasn't so close Blue would be tempted to take this into more than a hug—even though he knew he shouldn't. He inhaled her sweet tropical scent before reminding himself that he had to be more professional now. If she was hiring Red Stone, she was a job. Okay, she was a hell of a lot more than a job, but if he was going to be lead on her team, he had to act like it. And that meant not crossing any lines.

* * *

Mina sat on the bucket seat behind the wheel while the twin engine boat idled quietly in the water. Alex, who was currently inside the cabin, had been an impressive driver, clearly understanding the GPS system and everything else on the dashboard as he navigated them out to open water. She could steer a boat and that was about it. She also knew this particular vessel wasn't cheap so it was impressive the brothers had just let her and Alex take it out.

While she waited, Mina played with the hem of her dress as she fought her stupid internal battle. She hadn't been naked with a man in longer than she cared to admit and while she didn't plan to get naked now, her bathing suit was skimpier than her normal underclothes. Finally she just locked her insecurities up and slipped her dress over her head. She was going to have to take it off once they got to the reef so she might as well do it now.

She plucked the sunscreen from the cup holder next to Alex's bottle of water. He'd told her they were almost at their destination and even though it was weird to not be working during the day, it was a relief to get out of her condo. With the stress of kidnappers out there she wouldn't have wanted to be cooped up inside all day anyway.

Popping open the top of the bottle, she started smoothing sunscreen on her arms and legs, but kept scanning the area for any newcomers. She knew Alex was keeping watch too through the interior windows, probably more diligently than her, but she couldn't just not pay attention when she knew a threat was out there. Even if the threat had no clue where she was.

"Everything's all set." Alex's deep voice made her swivel toward the open cabin doors a few feet away from her. He stood there wearing plain blue swim trunks and nothing else. A rush of heat zipped up her spine as she drank in the sight of him. There couldn't be any fat on him. He was all sharp, cut lines and striations of perfection. The rise and fall of his chest was unsteady as he watched her. He wasn't looking below her neck, but it didn't matter. She might as well be naked for the hunger the man was emanating for her.

Instinctively she wrapped her arms around herself, feeling self-conscious. Maybe she shouldn't have taken her dress off. Now she was suddenly aware of how little clothing both of them had on—and how little restraint she had left when it came to Alex. She wished she could find the courage to make a move, but couldn't squash old insecurities.

Dispelling any ideas she might have to do just that, Alex looked away, his jaw tight. He rubbed a hand over his short hair. "We're almost to that reef if you want to grab some fins and a mask down below. I already laid mine out, but I wasn't sure what size your feet were." Without waiting for a response, he went to the wheel and gently moved the boat from neutral to drive, giving it a little gas as he steered them forward.

And that was that.

Feeling out of sorts, she stepped into the luxurious cabin and saw his fins and mask on the shiny wood tabletop of the dining area. Next to it was a small opening and stairs, likely leading to the stateroom. On that wall was a half-open door. She could see lifejackets and a mesh bag full of diving and snorkeling equipment. Good quality stuff, too.

After finding what she needed, she gathered both Alex's stuff and hers and headed back up top. As she stepped outside, he was slowing down. "Looks like we're not alone today."

Following his line of sight she saw there were five other boats, most were smaller than theirs, anchored in shallow looking water. "Is this the reef?"

"Yeah, Carter said mostly locals come here. We've got five known boats right now. If anyone else arrives and we don't like the way they look, we'll head out."

"That sounds good to me," she said as she set their masks and fins on the deck. "Would you mind putting sunscreen on my back?" She felt nervous asking, but she wasn't going to risk burning because of nerves.

Nodding, he cleared his throat as he retrieved the bottle. Turning, anticipation hummed through her as she waited to feel his big hands on her bare skin. She gathered her long hair together and pulled it to her front so it was out of his way. As the boat quietly idled, water lapped against the side of it, the salty scent permeating the air as she practically held her breath.

Lap, lap, lap.

It seemed an eternity passed before one of his hands smoothed lotion over the top of her back. She couldn't help it, she let out a little shudder at the feel of his callused fingers tracing over her. It didn't matter that there was nothing sexual about it, she liked him touching her. Heat flooded between her legs as he rubbed over her skin. Moving quickly, too quickly it seemed, he spread the sunscreen over her back, underneath the back tie of her top and over her shoulders. And was that her imagination or had his breathing increased too?

"All done," he rasped out. Oh yeah, he was definitely breathing harder.

When she turned around to face him, his back was to her. "Would you mind putting some on my back too?"

Swallowing hard, she nodded, then realized he couldn't see her. "No problem." She sounded a lot more steady than she felt. Her fingers actually shook as she squeezed the lotion into them. And when she started slathering it across the wide expanse of all those muscles, she had to actively stop herself from rubbing lower, lower... Her fingers skimmed the top of his swim trunks and she realized he was completely rigid. Like a statue.

"All done," she finally muttered as she practically shoved the bottle at him. Her face felt as if it were on fire. God, she'd been about to keep going until she felt all that deliciousness under his trunks. What was the matter with her? Had she actually planned to grab his ass and molest him? She needed to get herself under control now. This was simply sexual frustration. That's all. *Right.* Even she couldn't convince herself of that. It wasn't just any man who could make her react like this. No, it seemed Alex had turned her into this quivering mass of nerves.

Half-turning away from him, she scanned the wide open ocean again. Still just five boats. "Do we need to move in closer or are we good here?" At least her voice sounded steady when she asked.

"We're fine anchored here. It's all shallow and sandy-bottomed until it drops off into a reef. Look over the side. We can just walk to the reef." He didn't sound the least bit affected from her fingers on him, which made her feel stupid.

Unable to look at him, she grabbed her fins, mask and jumped over the side instead of using the back ladder. There was no point when it was so shallow, but mainly she just needed some distance from him. Fast. The clear blue water was warm, but still had a wonderful cooling effect on her overheated nerves. Ducking under, she savored the feel of the salty water and the sweltering sun overhead kissing her skin.

As she came out of it, Blue was standing right in front of her, the water coming up to his waist. She hadn't even heard him get in. Talk about stealth. She sucked in a quick breath at his close proximity. His eyes were unreadable as he watched her, but when his gaze briefly dipped to her breasts, she saw that flash of lust that mirrored her own. Just as quickly it was gone and disappointment flooded her. "Stay close, I don't want to be too far from the boat." His tone was brusque as he started wading through the water.

But she didn't take offense to it, she understood he was being vigilant. As they started heading for the reef two other boats roared up from the other direction and they both froze. The boats were too far away to see their occupants without binoculars and even though she doubted anyone knew where they were, a thread of panic twined through her.

"Come on." Alex took her hand and moved them toward the back of the boat. He tossed their fins and masks inside as they half swam, half walked to the ladder. "Let's just wait a minute," he murmured, his gaze on the newcomers who were moving closer and closer to where they were anchored.

The clear water around them grew choppier as they reached the back. Taking her by surprise, Alex grabbed her by the waist and set her up on the flat back area. But he barely glanced at her. Instead, he placed an almost absent hand on her knee, as if telling her to stay put, while he peered around the side of the boat.

A loud whooping sound made her stiffen in alarm, but just as quickly Alex let out a quiet laugh. Stepping back toward her, he placed both hands on either side of her legs, which were dangling in the water. "It's just a group of college-age kids. Two boatful's of them."

As if on cue, another loud shriek, then laughter, filled the air. Potent relief surged through her. Mina placed her hands on Alex's shoulders, unable to stop herself from slightly clenching around those muscles. "I don't need to see the reef. We can just hang out back here in the water and out of sight, soaking up some sun." She didn't want to have to hurry back to their boat every few minutes if a newcomer arrived. She also didn't want to leave completely. Being out here under the sun, with Alex, was relaxing and made the dark cloud hanging over her head not seem so scary.

His eyes darkened as he looked up at her. Beads of water dotted his face and hard jaw as he nodded jerkily. "Okay."

She frowned at his harsh tone. "What is it? Do you want to leave?"

He shook his head. "No, I want to kiss you." Her eyes widened at his blunt admission and that heat simmering inside her turned into a full-on flame. Before she could respond, he continued. "My attraction to you might cloud my judgment. I don't think it will, but if you'd like to remove me from your security detail when we arrive back on land, I understand. In fact, I think it's best if—"

Mina slid off the back dive board, and using the smooth glide of the water to give her momentum, slid her legs around his waist as she simultaneously wrapped her arms around his neck. She definitely didn't want him gone from her security detail. He was the only reason she wasn't a complete wreck right now. Alex made her feel safe. The water made a soft splashing sound against their bodies as they disturbed it.

His big body jerked in surprise, but he wound his arms around her, pulling her tight to his chest. "What are you doing?" he rasped out, his dark eyes inches from hers.

Oh, damn, she really wasn't good at this if he had to ask. "We're both attracted to each other?" It came out as more of a question even though she'd meant it as a statement.

He let out a harsh laugh and slid her down his muscular front until the juncture between her thighs slid right over his erection. Instinctively she tightened her legs around him.

Alex let out a shuddering groan. "Mina...we can't do anything. Not with me protecting you."

"But if you weren't protecting me? Officially?" She slowly grinded against him, grinning when he shuddered, his grip around her waist tightening as he pulled her even closer to him. Her inner walls tightened with an unfulfilled need. Just the feel of him against her body was enough to make her lose her mind.

He didn't answer though, just held her, watching her as if he couldn't figure out what to say. The feel of his muscular arms against her bare back sent shivers down her spine. There was hardly any clothing separating them and from the feel of his thick erection she could just imagine how good he would feel pumping inside her. Thrusting in and out.

Her nipples beaded tight as she rubbed against him again. Since he hadn't responded but also hadn't pushed her away, she took that as a good sign. Even though it was out of character for her to be so forward, she reached up and pulled the string on her bathing suit top free. She was tired of second guessing herself and being a coward. If she made this move and he rejected her, she'd just suffer the humiliation. Right now she didn't need any more words to show him what she wanted. She'd been too afraid to be bold last night and she'd regretted it all day. She didn't want any more regrets in her life, and knew she'd never regret Alex.

As the strings loosened and the triangles of cloth covering her breasts fell away, Alex's dark, hungry gaze dipped lower. His breathing was erratic and once again his grip tightened, as if he was afraid to let her go. She wasn't going anywhere. Because of how tightly they were pressed together, the triangles only slid down rather than off, still leaving her covered. Since Alex seemed almost frozen to the spot, she reached around to her back and released the other tie. Then she pulled away from him a few inches and tugged her top free.

He sucked in a sharp breath, his gaze seeming riveted to her pale pink nipples. They were beaded so tightly it was almost painful. "Mina..." Trailing off, he groaned when she arched herself into him, rubbing her breasts against his chest.

When he met her gaze she knew she'd won this little battle. He wasn't going to stop anything. Before she could take what she wanted, a taste of him, he crushed his mouth over hers like a man starving as he grinded his pelvis against hers.

His tongue danced and teased with hers, this kiss anything but simple. It felt like he was claiming her in some way. Everything about it was raw and unsteady and when he fisted a tight grip in her hair, she moaned at the unexpected bite of pleasure-pain.

One of his big hands held onto her hip as he moved them against the dive board. The second her spine connected with the back, that big hand cupped her breast, the callused pads of his fingers holding her almost reverently. His hold was so gentle, almost too gentle and in complete opposition to the hard grip on her hair and the erection pressed against her mound.

When his thumb started lightly stroking over her hard nipple, she moaned into his mouth. He rolled his hips against hers, his hard length stroking right over her pulsing clit. Their bathing suits did practically nothing to dull the sensations.

He groaned out her name as he pulled back and began kissing along her jaw and mouth. "You are so fucking beautiful, Mina."

She shuddered as he said her name again, loving the sound of it on his lips. For once she wasn't worried about a man wanting her for anything other than her. And she knew it wasn't just physical, though that was definitely a huge part of it.

As he nuzzled a sensitive spot along her neck he continued to tease her nipple, though he increased his pressure against the tight bud until she could hardly stand it. When he loosened his grip on her hair she was almost bereft, having found she liked that tight hold, but that faded when he reached between their bodies and started rubbing the heel of his palm against her mound, right over her clit.

"Oh, God." She arched into him, feeling like a damn teenager with out of control hormones. Needing to feel him too, she slid one of her hands down his chest, tracing all the muscular lines and striations before dipping into his swim trunks. The moment she fisted his thick length, he jerked against her, his teeth nipping her shoulder.

Feeling almost possessed with the need to make him come, she started stroking him. When she tightened her grip it was easy to tell how much he liked it.

Growling against her shoulder, he continued a path down to her other breast. With no teasing or build up, he sucked her hard nipple into his mouth.

Everything around them seemed to fade away as he continued pleasuring her with his hands and mouth. The pressure on her mound hadn't lessened and even though he wasn't using his fingers, just grinding against her clit, it was more than enough stimulation.

Surprisingly so.

Taking her by surprise, he pressed down on both her nipples, lightly pinching one with his fingers and the other between his teeth. The erotic action pushed her straight into orgasm, the pleasure flowing out to all her nerves with the intensity of a battering ram. She buried her face against his chest, raking her teeth against him as she cried out.

As her climax punched through her, she tightened her hold around his cock, pumping him faster and harder. It was as if her release set him free. With a growl of need, he pulled her head back again and sought out her mouth, his tongue flicking against hers as they both found their release.

Her orgasm seemed to go on forever, until finally she withdrew her hand and sagged against his body, thankful for the buoyancy of the water as her shaking legs fell from around him. When she met his gaze, he looked just as stunned as she felt. Even though she was feeling sated, it was as if that climax had only taken the edge off. She wanted to feel him inside her, filling her as he moved.

As his breathing returned to normal, his big hands landed on her hips, pulling her close in a way she could never mistake for anything other than possessive. "That was..."

For a moment panic filled her as he seemed to struggle with himself. If he said what had just happened was a mistake she didn't know what she'd do. "Amazing," she whispered, finishing for him.

He nodded, eyes smoldering. "And we're just getting started." The dark edge to his voice made her think he was walking a tightrope of control.

And she couldn't help but wonder what would happen if she pushed him off it.

CHAPTER EIGHT

Blue couldn't believe what they'd just done. What *he'd* just done. Fuck. He wanted to kick his own ass. Now that the blood had rushed back to his brain, he glanced around the open water then peered around the back of the boat again.

Nothing had changed so he allowed a small bit of relief to slide through him as he looked back at Mina.

Her dark green eyes were brighter against the ocean water as she tied her top back on. She looked sated, but nervous. Probably because he hadn't said anything else. He cleared his throat, trying to find the right words.

Her cheeks flushed pink as he watched her, but at least she reached for him again, holding onto his shoulders in a light grip. Her touch seemed to ground him. "So that wasn't just a onetime thing, right?" she asked, her voice so quiet he barely heard her over the soft waves lapping against the side of the boat.

He knew he should say that it had been. This was against protocol and even if it wasn't, it still wasn't professional. He'd never done anything like this since working for Red Stone. And even in the Marines he'd had to be careful about who he got involved with since he was an officer. He'd pretty much given up sex when he'd been on a tour overseas. He hadn't been willing to risk his career on the off chance that a woman lied about her rank or who she was attached to. He'd usually found a willing woman when he was back from duty. And if he didn't, his fist had always worked fine.

Now... "No. Not a onetime thing." There was no way in hell he could walk away from her. "But I need to disclose to my boss that we're...involved."

Her face turned an even brighter shade of red as she shook her head. The ends of her wet hair swayed against her now covered breasts, making him want to push the material away and suck the still hard buds into his mouth again. "No way. What if they try to remove you from my detail?" As she said the words, her face fell and she stiffened. The movement was slight but he didn't miss it. "I mean, unless that's what you want."

After what they'd just done her insecurity surprised the hell out of him. As her hands started to fall from his shoulders, he covered them, holding her fingers against his chest. "I definitely don't want that. And you're the client. Under normal circumstances Harrison would have a problem with this. And truthfully, he'll have a problem with it now, but I'm pretty sure he'll make an exception for you."

She raised a dark eyebrow. "Because of my father?"

"Yeah." Harrison was a businessman and wouldn't try to remove him if Mina insisted on his presence. Or he hoped his boss wouldn't. Because Blue wasn't sure he'd give a shit what Harrison said when it came to this woman.

Her entire body relaxed then. "So..." The spark of desire in her eyes hadn't disappeared and now it seemed to have taken on a life of its own. The hungry way she looked at him made him want to throw caution away, shove her bikini bottom to the side and sink deep inside her.

Almost.

Her safety mattered more than their own needs, though. "I need to check my phone to see if Carter's called with any updates. And I need to check in with Harrison. He's getting a team put together now but they won't be here until this afternoon. I want to get an ETA on their arrival so we can meet them. If we can swing it, we'll have dinner with Carter and Chris before we head back to your place."

Disappointment flared in her eyes, but she nodded. "Okay."

He couldn't stand disappointing her. "I want you more than I've wanted anyone. Ever." The words tore from him on a ragged growl. He couldn't even pretend not to be affected by her. "It's taking all my restraint not to take you up to the stateroom and fuck you until neither of us can walk. But I can't put you at risk. As soon as we're alone, however..." He trailed off, not able to say the words. The more he talked or thought about fucking her, the more he wanted to make it a reality.

Eyes wide, she nodded and a pleased smile danced across her full lips. "I'm glad I'm not the only one who feels this crazy chemistry. I can't believe I came so fast." She said the last part as if she was embarrassed.

He couldn't guess why though. It had been insanely hot to feel her writhing against him like that when he hadn't even penetrated her. Imagining how much more intense it would be for her, for *both* of them, when he finally sank deep inside her made his half-hard cock start to lengthen again. Shit. Now was not the time for that.

* * *

Lewis glanced at Harry as his crew member slowed their vehicle. He was cautiously steering down the road that led to the small but exclusive Key West neighborhood their person of interest lived in. His DMV contact had gotten back to him and the owner of the truck was a man named Chris Foley. So far he hadn't found out much about him other than he and his brother owned a well-known dive shop.

And Lewis needed more information before he went in anywhere blind.

"We could attempt to park somewhere else and go over one of the walls. Do it around dusk," Harry said as he turned, slowed and pulled a U-turn instead of driving all the way up to the guarded gatehouse.

Lewis shook his head as he went over their options. "Not until we know more about this Foley."

"They could just be friends. If the guy lives here he's clearly doing well for himself."

"Yeah, maybe. But she hasn't had any contact with him since we've been watching her. I don't like his sudden appearance in her life."

Harry nodded and turned onto the next quiet street.

"Head to his dive shop. I want to see if he's there."

"Why?"

"I just do. I want to get a feel for the guy." You could tell a lot about someone from talking to them.

And if the guy was at work, but his truck was at the Hollingsworth woman's house, that just left more questions. Maybe they could get to the woman through Foley. From his driver's license picture Lewis knew it wasn't the man who'd saved her, but it was possible they could find either a connection to Mina or to the man from the alley through Foley. It was worth a shot and Lewis believed in being over-prepared for these jobs.

"Fine, whatever," Harry muttered.

Lewis looked out the window, contemplating whether this job that was originally supposed to be an easy grab and bag was going to be more hassle than it was worth. If the price on the woman's head wasn't so high, he might seriously consider walking away from it.

But there was no way he could back out now.

Besides, even if he wanted to he doubted the rest of the crew would bail. They'd all put in time and effort and only been paid half until the job was done. No one was going anywhere until they collected their final due.

CHAPTER NINE

"We'll be there in a couple minutes," Carter said from the front seat of his SUV as he drove Blue and Mina back to her place.

Mina was stretched out on top of Blue as they lay on the floorboards and he couldn't get enough of her. While he more than appreciated Carter's help, he wished he and Mina were alone and with a lot less clothing in the way.

They were entering the garage the same way they'd left and no one should be any wiser that they'd been gone all day. Not unless the would-be kidnappers had cameras set up in the garage or had somehow tapped into the live feeds of the ones run by the management company who owned the building. But neither Blue nor Carter had seen anything when they'd searched.

Chris had been sitting on the condo but they'd had an emergency at work with one of their staff nearly slicing his hand clean off on one of the motors. So Carter's brother was now at the hospital with the guy and they'd shut down early. And Carter would be heading there himself as soon as he dropped Blue and Mina off.

"Thanks," Blue said, not in a big rush to have Mina move off him. Every time they took a turn and she shifted over him, he had to fight a groan at the feel of her tight body on his.

They'd spent the last few hours on the boat and he could tell it had done a world of good for her. She seemed a hundred times more at ease since yesterday. He knew she wouldn't be completely relaxed until whoever wanted her kidnapped was caught, but he could see the difference and was glad for it. They hadn't done anything more than kiss the rest of the day because he hadn't been willing to lose focus, but things between them had been easy even if the day had been sexually charged. The kisses had been sensual, but they'd both held back.

Mina wiggled over him, grinning wickedly as she moved over his erection. He'd been like that since she'd climbed on top of him back at Carter's place.

"You're gonna pay for that," he said under his breath, for her ears only, as he cupped her butt and rolled his hips against hers.

She let out a soft moan. "I hope so." Her words were a breathy whisper. The wicked note in her voice was unmistakable, making him even harder. Something he hadn't thought possible.

"I can hear you guys," Carter muttered from the front.

Grinning, Mina buried her face against Blue's neck and stifled a laugh. Under other circumstances he might be embarrassed that anyone could hear them, especially since he was on a job, but Carter was his friend and wouldn't judge. Wrapping his arms around her, Blue tightened his grip until he felt his phone buzz in his pocket. He'd changed back into cargo pants and a T-shirt once they'd returned to Carter's place. Mina shifted to the side so he could grab it.

"Blue, here," he said, all business since it was Harrison on the other end.

"Where are you guys?"

"Pulling up to her place any minute."

"The team's been slightly delayed. There was an accident right on the Seven Mile Bridge so they're about an hour out. They could probably make it faster on foot." Harrison let out an annoyed curse. "I should have just flown them down."

The drive was so short and even a private flight would have taken longer for them to get clearance so Blue knew why he hadn't. "It's fine. Her place is secure. I'll keep it locked down...Unless there's something you're not telling me?"

On top of him, Mina stiffened, but he didn't look at her, needing to keep his focus on Harrison.

"Lizzy just found something during one of her searches. Could be nothing, but she spotted the same man near Mina's condo more than once and near your friend's dive shop. Don't know if he went inside or not because the cameras she was able to access have limited angles."

Blue knew that Lizzy, wife of one of the owners, had used her very illegal hacking skills to scan faces via CCTVs she'd linked into through open wireless connections. Then she'd run the faces through a facial recognition software program the company had. He didn't know if that program was legal and he'd never asked because he didn't care what the answer was.

"She couldn't get a face shot of him near the condo because he was wearing a hat there, but I'm positive it's the same man. He's got the same build and is wearing the same clothes. And, more telling than anything, he took a picture of Chris's truck. It was slick, but we got him doing it."

"And?" Blue tried to temper his impatience, knowing Harrison needed to give him all relevant details.

"Guy's name is Lewis Hudgins. There were a couple pings on his name but he doesn't have a record. Unfortunately he's been linked as a person of interest to at least a dozen high-profile kidnappings. The Feds want this guy bad, but no one's ever been able to make charges stick. He works one big job a year and uses a different crew each time."

So even if they wanted to hunt this guy down using his partners it would be impossible since he didn't have a standard team. "You know where he is now?"

"No. Wherever he's staying, he's not using a credit card in his name and Lizzy lost him on one of the feeds and his face hasn't resurfaced yet. I'll send you his picture."

"All right, I'll show it to Mina, see if she recognizes him. Has Lizzy found any financials linking him to...anyone?" Meaning whatever fuckhead had hired the guy and his crew to take Mina. He just didn't want to say that in front of her.

"No. There's a reason the Feds have never been able to pin anything on him. We'll keep her safe though. And you'll have backup soon. Get her inside and under lockdown."

"Will do. I'll keep you updated if anything changes. What about that other thing Lizzy's looking into?" Blue closed his eyes as he spoke, purposefully not meeting Mina's gaze. The SUV had slowed and the interior went darker so he knew they'd entered her private garage.

"It's like the guy's a ghost," Harrison said quietly, maybe guessing that Mina was nearby. "He's not at his home in California and even my father can't get hold of him. We're going to keep trying though."

"Thanks." Blue knew Mina was starting to get worried that she hadn't heard back from her dad or his head of security so he'd asked Harrison to try to hunt both men down. What his boss had just told him, however, was worrisome.

"The garage is empty," Carter said as the vehicle pulled to a stop. "You guys are good."

"What did Harrison say?" Mina asked as she sat up.

Blue immediately missed the feel of her, but locked that thought down. He needed to get her upstairs. "The team's a little delayed. Car accident on the bridge. But they'll be here soon. They also might have a lead on one of the guys looking to take you. Harrison's sending me a picture for you to look at."

Face pinched, she nodded. "What else did you ask him about? You were avoiding my gaze when you asked him that last thing."

Yeah, he should have known she wouldn't let that go. Damn, she was perceptive. "Red Stone is looking into contacting your father. I just didn't want to tell you until they'd found something." He hadn't wanted to get her hopes up in case they failed.

She must have understood because her expression softened. "Thanks, Alex."

Before he could respond, Carter cleared his throat from the front. Immediately Blue went into battle mode. "We need to get you upstairs." They hadn't brought much with them except clothes and a few snacks for the day so he grabbed their bag.

"We're clear," Carter said, hand on the door handle.

Blue trusted him, but did another visual scan before retrieving his weapon from the bag. Normally he wore it on him but hadn't wanted to with Mina stretched out over him. "Let's go," he murmured, getting out before Mina.

There were only two cars in the small garage so there was nowhere for anyone to hide. Still, Blue moved in front of Mina while Carter moved in behind her, boxing her in as they strode to the elevator. Hyperaware, Blue didn't let his guard down even when they'd made it safely inside the elevator and it was heading upward. It didn't surprise him that Carter had decided to ride up with them as backup.

When they stepped out onto the third floor, Mina's phone started a soft dinging sound. Since she was wearing another summer dress he'd put her phone in his pocket. As he went to grab it, the elevator shut behind them but Mina froze, her hand clutching Blue's upper arm. "That's my phone's alarm," she whispered, her expression tense. "It means someone's in my condo..." She trailed off as the dinging stopped. "They put the wrong alarm code in, it's why it went off, but they must have entered the right one because it stopped."

As a jolt of adrenaline surged through him, Blue held up a finger to his lips then pulled out a backup pistol from his ankle holster. He handed it and her phone to her and motioned to the end of the hallway. "Call the police," he whispered. "If anything happens to us, use that gun if you have to, but try to get away. Use the stairs."

Clutching the phone to her chest and the weapon at her side she nodded and hurried out of the way, her sandals softly slapping against the tile. There was no time to comfort her or go over anything. He and Carter needed to get in there now. He couldn't take the risk there was a backup crew downstairs waiting to ambush them.

Carter had his own weapon out, a SIG similar to the one Blue had in hand. Blue motioned that he was going to use Mina's key to unlock the door, but when he tried the handle he found it open.

He hated going into any situation blind, but there was no choice. He couldn't hear any noise coming from inside and had no clue how many men might be in there. The good thing was, he and Carter should have the element of surprise.

Moving quietly, he pushed the door open with his foot, keeping his weapon up and ready. The interior hallway was empty. Sweeping inside, he moved down the hall on silent feet, staying close to the east wall while Carter was flush against the west one.

As they reached the end they both instinctively slowed then stopped. Blue leaned back against his side, peering into part of the kitchen and he had a full view of the living room. Empty. He looked at Carter who had a view of part of the hallway and the mini-library.

Carter shook his head, his blue eyes completely focused. Blue lifted his hand, ready to motion that they should sweep down to the bedrooms when he heard a man talking. He tensed, remaining in place.

"She's not here. No..." A sigh of frustration. "I'm just going to try calling her again." The voice grew closer as the man headed down the hallway toward them.

Blue shifted back so he could extend out his weapon and Carter did the same. The man continued talking and the second he came into their line of sight both Carter and Blue stepped out.

The blond haired man went still, his eyes betraying a flicker of surprise, but other than that he didn't move.

"Put your fucking phone down *now*," Blue said quietly. "Just drop it. And don't make any sudden moves."

"Where's Mina?" the man asked even as he did what Blue ordered, letting his cell tumble from his fingers.

The familiar way he said her name was jarring but Blue didn't care. "Put your hands on top of your head slowly and get to your knees. Don't attempt to draw your weapon or we'll put you down. You alone?" Blue couldn't actually see a weapon but if the way the man gritted his teeth was any indication, he was definitely armed.

Carter moved out to the left, slowly circling the guy as he continued following orders. Sheathing his weapon in the back of his pants, Carter started patting the guy down. After pulling out two guns and two blades, he tossed them into Mina's library before withdrawing his SIG again.

The man still hadn't answered Blue's question so he kept his weapon pinned on him while Carter moved back to the bedrooms. A couple minutes later he returned. "All clear," he murmured, taking up position behind the unknown man.

"If you've hurt her I'll fucking gut you," the man's words were a guttural growl, the anger in his gaze clear.

Blue frowned, flicking a gaze to Carter before looking back at the other man. "Who are you? Why are you here?"

The man's jaw tightened, as if he wasn't going to respond, but then he said, "Ivan Mitchell. Head of her father's security. Where the hell is she?"

Gun hand steady, Blue pulled out his cell with his other hand and brought up the picture Harrison had sent of Lewis Hudgins. It was a different man than the one in front of him now. "Mina?" he shouted without turning around.

He heard her shoes slapping loudly against the tile now as she hurried to her condo. "I've called the police. They're on their way," she said as she came up behind him. Out of the corner of his eye Blue saw her jerk abruptly to a halt. "Ivan? What are you doing here? I've been trying to call you!"

The man started to lower his arms but Blue shook his head. "Don't fucking move."

Thankfully Mina didn't say anything, just stared at the man as she waited for answers.

Ivan nodded his head at Blue but didn't take his eyes off her. "Who are these guys?"

"My security," she said without pause.

He nodded again, seeming relieved by that. So maybe the guy wasn't involved with her would-be kidnapping but Blue wasn't letting his guard down until he had answers. "Start talking. We want to know why the hell you haven't been returning her calls and why you're in her condo uninvited. How did you know her security code?"

"I guessed your code, Mina," he said, keeping his focus on her while ignoring Blue. His expression turned admonishing. "I didn't realize you had a system, but I got it in two tries. Not smart."

Mina let out a growl of frustration. "Really? A lecture now! Some assholes tried to kidnap me and thanks to the kindness of a stranger I'm okay. I've been trying to call you and my dad since last night. What the hell is going on?"

It was the first time Blue had seen Mina lose her temper, and the situation withstanding, he liked it.

"I didn't get your messages until a couple hours ago and I've tried calling you back. Multiple times. It kept going to voicemail."

"Bullshit," Mina snapped. She looked at her phone, then frowned as she turned toward Blue, talking under her breath so only he could hear. "I actually didn't have any bars on the water. It's possible he tried then."

Blue nodded, his focus laser sharp. "So why are you here? When did you arrive? And why hasn't Mina's father called her?"

Ivan looked at Blue, his gaze assessing. "I'm here because her father sent me and I arrived about ten minutes ago by helicopter. Came in straight from Miami where Warren is staying. He hasn't called because..." His expression softened as he flicked a glance at Mina. "Shit, there's no way to break this to you gently. It's why I'm here in person. He's dying, Mina."

Next to him Mina gasped. "What?"

"Pancreatic cancer. By the time he was diagnosed it was already too advanced. If they'd caught it a year ago he might have had a chance, but..." Ivan looked down, the pain in his expression real enough that Blue believed he cared. "He's got a few weeks left. It's why he's in Miami. He'd like to spend his time with you so he moved closer."

Mina reached out and clutched onto Blue's forearm for support. Blue didn't miss the way Ivan zeroed in on that touch, but he didn't care what the other man made of it. Keeping his weapon steady, he wrapped his free arm around Mina, who sagged into him. "Why didn't he call me sooner? I would have just come home."

"He was diagnosed less than a week ago and you know your dad. He does things his way, decided he wanted to see the east coast and more importantly, you, so we made it happen. He...it's bad, Mina." Ivan's jaw tightened.

"You can put your guns down," Mina said quietly, but neither Blue nor Carter moved.

"Not until you talk to your father. For all we know he's involved in the kidnapping attempt." Blue didn't care if the guy seemed sincere. He wasn't taking a risk with her safety.

"Are you fucking kidding me? What would I have to gain by kidnapping her?" Ivan's voice was incredulous.

Carter snorted from behind Ivan. "A lot of fucking money."

Mina shook her head and placed a firm hand on Blue's chest as she burrowed tighter against him. From the look on Ivan's face he didn't like that at all. Interesting. "He's paid very well, Alex. He wouldn't be involved in this, trust me. Even if I didn't know how much he makes, I know he wouldn't do something like this to me. Please trust me."

There was such a strong note of conviction in her voice that Blue was tempted to lower his weapon. But his judgment wasn't clouded. Before he could respond, his phone buzzed in his hand. Since his arm was wrapped around Mina he held it palm up. He flicked a quick glance at it, not wanting to take his eyes off Ivan, but he knew Carter wouldn't let the guy make a move anyway.

Swiping his thumb across the screen, he typed in his code and pulled up the text from Harrison. *Team twenty minutes out. New development. Ivan Mitchell linked to Lewis Hudgins. Don't let Mina call him again or let her know.*

Shit. Too late for that. Blue wouldn't have opened the damn text in front of her if he'd suspected a message like that. Mina looked up at him, her green eyes wide and disbelieving. Blue shook his head, warning her not to say anything. Unwrapping his arm from around her, he slowly moved her behind him. "Carter, I need your keys." True to form, Carter tossed them over without question. "Stay with him until the police arrive. I'll put in a call and let them know you're here keeping him de-tained." Because he was getting Mina the hell out of there. If Ivan was involved with any of this, he didn't want her anywhere near him. For all Blue knew, the bastard was lying about her dad to play on her sympathy.

Ivan cursed and started to move, but froze when Carter let out a vicious threat.

"I owe you, man." Blue said, backing up to the door, but half-turning so he had a visual of the hallway as they exited.

"Just call me when you can," Carter said. "Let me know you're safe."

"I will. I'm also going to need another transportation favor." Blue didn't voice the question but raised his eyebrows instead, knowing his friend would understand.

Carter nodded. "No problem. You better gas it up before you return it though."

A smile tugged at his lips as he continued their exit. Blue planned to head right back to Carter's place and use his boat as a means of escape from Key West. He wasn't using the roads or trying the private airport because if Ivan was involved it stood to reason that maybe more of her father's men were too. Maybe they were taking advantage of the man when he was sick. Or maybe he wasn't sick at all but under duress somewhere. For all Blue knew they were staked out at the airport or had even staged that accident delaying the Red Stone team. The probability of that happening was exceedingly slim, but Blue didn't give a shit.

He was getting Mina out of town as fast as possible.

CHAPTER TEN

A s soon as Blue hung up with Harrison, Mina said, "Ivan is *not* involved with this. I don't care what proof your team has."

Blue's jaw tightened as he glanced in the rearview mirror. They'd left ten minutes ago and didn't appear to have a tail, but he wasn't taking that chance. He'd contacted the police—who'd been pissed they'd left Mina's condo without staying to talk to them—and Harrison. His boss had filled him in on the phone records Lizzy had found connecting Ivan to Lewis Hudgins, including a call a couple hours ago. Probably right before Ivan had left for Key West from Miami. Maybe he had planned to lure Mina out but hadn't counted on her having security of her own. While the evidence wouldn't amount to much in a court, it was damning enough for Blue to take action.

"The evidence doesn't lie, sweetheart." The endearment just slipped out, but it felt natural. He kept his voice soft, knowing she was dealing with a lot considering the recent knowledge of her father's condition.

Harrison had also confirmed that Warren Hollingsworth was in Miami and dying. It hadn't hit the news yet, but Harrison's father—who was former CIA and had more contacts than Blue could imagine—had reached out to some associates and discovered the news while Blue had been holding Ivan at gunpoint. Blue really wished it weren't true. Even if Mina's relationship with her father was strained, it was clear this was tearing her up.

"But I know him. He loves my father." Mina's voice cracked as she turned to look out the window.

Blue didn't know what to say. Feeling out of his depth, he kept his gaze on the road and their surroundings. The silence between them stretched, growing almost painful. He wanted to reach out to her, to comfort her, but wasn't sure how. When his phone buzzed again he answered it gratefully. "Yeah."

"Hey, just got off the phone with Harrison. The team and I are on our way to that address you gave him. How do you want to play this?" It was Vincent, ex-SEAL, highly trained Red Stone security agent and one of Blue's best friends.

He was grateful Harrison had assigned Vincent to this op. "We'll take my friend's boat straight to home base. Harrison's making arrangements for us to dock somewhere private and close to the safe house." Even though he doubted anyone could overhear their conversation he kept details to a minimum. It was second nature to him. "Harrison's getting a team in place at her father's house. Once he's sure the place is secure we'll move her from the safe house to his place."

"Sounds good. See you in fifteen."

The second he disconnected, Mina asked, "I'll get to see my father tonight then?"

"Yes. We're going to do everything to get you to him. We just need to check out his security team and the house first. And, our guys will be in place the entire time you're there." Because they weren't depending on her father's men. Not when it looked like Ivan Mitchell was involved with Mina's attempted kidnapping.

Surprising him, she reached out and squeezed his arm. "Thank you for everything. I know you're doing your job but...just, thank you."

He stole a glance at her. "You don't have to thank me. Ever. And you're more than a job, Mina." Admitting that took a hell of a lot. He'd never put himself out there for a woman. Had never wanted to. But Mina was different. Looking away, he focused on the road even though he wanted to pull over, find somewhere private and comfort her. Having lost his own brother, he knew how hard it was to lose a loved one.

Mina didn't respond and for that he was grateful. He glanced in the rearview mirror again as he turned down the last street before they would reach Carter's gated neighborhood. The street they were on now wasn't gated, but the long row of similarly built two-story pastel homes was prime real estate. Considering how small Key West was, pretty much everything here was prime.

He frowned, his adrenaline increasing when a van without its lights on pulled out from a side street behind them. There weren't any cars on the road and the sun had just set so it was possible the driver hadn't turned on the lights yet. Still, he wasn't taking any chances. Since he couldn't turn around now without a risk of boxing them in, he sped up a fraction, keeping his attention divided between the road in front of him and the van behind them.

"Don't turn around and don't panic but we might have a tail. There's nowhere else we can go but to Carter's." He handed her his cell phone. "Call the last number I received a call from. His name is Vincent and he's part of your new team. Tell him we might have a tail and to keep the line open." Because Blue couldn't talk to him when he might have to do some quick maneuvering. And he didn't have his earpiece with him to give him hands-free capability.

She sucked in a breath, her expression startled, but to Mina's credit she didn't question him, just took the phone and dialed. The van behind him hadn't sped up any but Blue wasn't taking a chance. He reached for the small keyfob attached to Carter's keychain and pressed the button to open the gate. They were still about thirty yards out but he could see it starting to open. The gate was new too so as he reached the ten yard mark, it was fully open.

The van behind them jerked ahead, as if the driver realized what Blue was doing.

Gunning it, Blue took a sharp turn into the quiet neighborhood. Since he'd opened the gate himself and he was driving Carter's SUV he doubted the guard in the small gatehouse would attempt to stop him. Not that he cared.

Short of the guard shooting his tires out, Blue wasn't slowing down. Next to him Mina was relaying everything to Vincent with a shaky voice, but at least she was remaining calm.

As he shot through the gate, he pressed the button to close it. After a few seconds' delay it started to close. For a brief moment Blue wondered if he'd overreacted but when the van came into view, racing straight for the gate, a jolt of pure adrenaline surged through him.

"We're going to park and make a run for the boat. Get ready," he told Mina. There was no other exit and since he didn't want to get into a gun battle with their pursuers, escaping was the only choice.

She nodded and murmured what was going on to Vincent before un-strapping her seatbelt. Blue shot a glance in the rearview mirror again. The van slammed into the gate before it could fully close, sending it flying off its hinges.

They had a good lead, but Blue's grip on the steering wheel tightened. By now the security guard would have already called the police but even if they dispatched this second they'd never arrive in time to help. Neither would the Red Stone team.

"Alex." Mina sounded terrified as he neared Carter's home.

"We're going to make it." He sounded more confident than he felt.

A look in the rearview mirror gave him a small burst of relief. It looked as if the van had totaled out after ramming the gate. Those fuckers would have to come after them on foot.

Mina turned around and he could practically feel the terror rolling off her. Which made him want to pummel the shit out of each and every one of the men involved in this.

"Don't look back," he ordered as he made the sharp turn into Carter's driveway. "Get ready to go. Jump out and follow me as soon as I park."

Seconds later, he slowed then stopped completely, the SUV shuddering under the abrupt stop. Mina's door was open before Blue had his thrown open. As he flew from the vehicle, he withdrew his weapon. When there was time to slow down he'd give Mina his backup but now he couldn't risk it. "This way," he said quietly as she rounded the front of the vehicle to meet him.

They sprinted toward the side of the house, but he held back a foot so that she was in front of him. He only risked a quick glance over his shoulder as they rounded the side of it. No one was there. Yet. But he knew they were coming.

To try such a bold kidnapping meant they were desperate. That didn't bode well for either of them. The more desperate they got, the higher the chance of someone getting hurt.

Thankfully there wasn't a privacy fence. Not in a neighborhood like this. There were big hedges separating the homes, but a stone walkway led them straight back to the pool area. Breathing erratically, Mina kept pace as they raced past the pool and down the dock beyond it.

Blue couldn't hear their pursuers but that was almost worse. "When we reach the boat, start the engine. I'll untie the ropes."

He thought she might argue, but instead she nodded as he handed the keys to her. Their shoes pounded loudly against the wooden dock, but Blue kept his focus. Mina jumped directly onto the back dive board area, her hands shaking as she opened the small back door leading to the stern of the vessel.

Though he hated to set his weapon down for any reason, he tucked it into his waistband as he hurriedly untied the first rope. Mina had already started the boat so all he had to was untie the second.

"Don't let them leave!" a man shouted.

Blue didn't look up as he worked fast, not wanting to get the rope tangled and slow them down. "Put it in drive. Move the lever forward," he said, loud enough for Mina to hear.

When a shot rent the air and wood splintered near the front of the dock, his head snapped up and he pulled out his weapon. "Gun it!" he ordered, leaving the last of the rope attached.

The boat jerked forward as Blue lifted his weapon. He quickly assessed the situation. He could only see two men advancing, but he didn't doubt there were more coming. Both were near the pool and getting closer. One raised his weapon. Blue fired at him, aiming for dead center. The man dropped where he stood as the Hatteras kicked up a huge wake, pulling away from the dock.

Another shot echoed in the night air as Blue turned and raced down the dock. The rope was quickly losing slack as the boat pulled farther away. His leg muscles strained as he dove for the back of it. He landed on his feet but tumbled back as Mina pressed the lever down even harder.

Before he'd pushed up he heard the cracking of the dock ripping under the pressure. Weapon in hand, he grabbed the side of the boat and stood, ready to return fire but didn't have to. A man stood at the front of the dock, but the rest of it had caved under the pressure of the Hatteras.

Even though he and Mina were far enough away to be out of firing distance, Blue kept his weapon raised as he walked backward to her. "How're you doing?"

"Fantastic. I do this kind of shit every day." There was a frantic quality to her voice as she let out a shaky laugh.

Despite what had just happened, Blue chuckled, still not taking his gaze off the kidnappers. "Yeah well, you handled yourself impressively."

She snorted. "That's because I'm in shock."

Now that they'd pulled far enough away, he risked a glance at her. Even with just the moonlight illuminating them, he could see how pale she was. "I need to pull the rest of the rope in and dislodge whatever is left of the dock, but then I'll take over. Do you know how to use the electrical panel? We need lights now that we're in open water."

She looked at him, her eyes wide, but her expression was determined as she nodded. "I've got this."

Though he wanted to pull her into his arms, kiss her until she was breathless, and reassure her that everything would be okay, he moved into action, securing the last of the rope. Carter wouldn't care about the damages, but Blue would pay for them. He'd dragged his friend into this and he wasn't letting Red Stone cover it.

As soon as he'd finished, he joined Mina. While she drove he typed their destination into the GPS system. Unless these kidnappers had a speed boat or helicopter waiting, then he and Mina were in the clear until they reached Miami. Of course then they'd have a shitload of stuff to deal with because Blue was almost positive the man he'd shot was dead. Which meant he'd have to head back to Key West to make a statement to the police. But he wasn't leaving Mina anytime soon.

* * *

Mina splashed water on her face before turning off the bathroom faucet. She knew they'd be reaching Miami soon and couldn't stop the nerves from jangling around in her stomach. Everything that had happened in the last couple days had her head spinning. Thank God for Alex's presence. It still stunned her how this stranger had come out of nowhere and now meant so incredibly much to her. After patting her face dry, she stepped out of the small, luxury bathroom to find Alex sitting on the edge of the king-size bed in the stateroom.

"What are you doing?" she asked, worry lancing through her since they shouldn't have docked yet.

"Harrison and a small team just boarded. They wanted to ride in with us the rest of the way to the marina. We'll be there in about five minutes. You've been down here a while so I wanted to check on you." He watched her carefully, as if he was afraid she was going to have a breakdown.

She figured if she was going to have one she'd have full-on melted down by now. "I'm good. Just stressed about seeing my dad and worrying about what I'm going to say to him about Ivan. I...I don't think I'm going to say anything just yet. Not until the police have figured out more." Her father was already dying. Telling him now would kill him faster.

"According to Harrison he's still being detained and questioned. Still denying everything too." There was a barely concealed note of disgust in Alex's voice.

Mina pulled her lips into a thin line as she sat next to him. She knew she was likely being an idiot by believing in Ivan but her gut told her that he wasn't involved. It just didn't fit with what she knew of his character. "Have they found a reason he could be involved? And don't say money because I don't buy that. I mean, maybe gambling debts or something?" Not that she'd excuse him if he did have debts. Hell no. Not after someone had tried to kidnap her and taken shots at both her and Alex. But she wanted to understand how someone she'd known for years, someone she trusted, could do something like this.

Alex shook his head. "No, but they're pulling apart his financials. They haven't got the kidnappers to talk yet, but they will."

He sounded so confident she had to believe the police would eventually get to the bottom of everything. Even though the men from the dock had tried to escape, the Red Stone team had arrived not long after and detained the men until the police arrived. "What's going to happen to you because of the shooting?" Mina knew the man he'd shot had died. It might have been in self-defense and justifiable but she also knew Alex would have to talk to the police about it.

"Don't worry about that."

He wasn't being condescending but the statement still annoyed her. She placed a hand on his knee and squeezed. "Seriously? Don't worry?"

His lips tugged up into a half-smile. "I just mean, it will work itself out. Right now you need to focus on seeing your father. The team is going to take you to him immediately. The house and security team has been vetted well enough. Not enough to make Harrison or me a hundred percent happy, but...we'll be with you the whole time and you should be with your father."

The urgent note in his voice told her everything she needed to know. "It's bad?"

Alex nodded. "Yeah...I'm so sorry sweetheart."

This was the second time Alex had used that endearment and it completely disarmed her. Especially now when she was feeling raw and vulnerable. If they were taking her directly to her father she knew what that meant. Her throat tightened and she closed her eyes, fighting the onslaught of tears. When she'd called her dad earlier, his doctor had answered. The man had been kind, but had said her father couldn't talk because of the pain meds he was on. As she started to dash away escaping tears, Alex pulled her into a tight embrace. She wrapped her arms around him and buried her face against his neck while he rubbed a gentle hand down her spine. He murmured soothing sounds that did little to dull her pain, but she was so grateful for his presence.

"Whatever happens, I'm here for you," he said against her hair.

Mina nodded and held on tight. Having Alex with her made all the difference in the world. So much so that she couldn't even imagine her life without him in it now.

CHAPTER ELEVEN

Blue rubbed a hand over his head, a nervous habit he had. Right now he didn't give a shit how obvious it was he was worried. He'd already told Harrison he was involved with Mina and had removed himself from her personal detail. It didn't mean he was removing himself from her life. He didn't need the damn money from this job and nothing could tear him away from her except Mina herself.

"She's strong, man," Vincent murmured next to him. "Look how well she's held up under all this. She'll be okay."

Blue nodded tightly, unable to look at his friend. Instead he stared straight ahead at the wall in front of him. He, Vincent and the majority of the twelve man Red Stone Security team—including Harrison, Porter and Grant Caldwell—were waiting in the hall outside Warren Hollingsworth's room. Blue shouldn't be surprised the three brothers were all here but it had stunned him initially to see them. Mina was a high priority for them though, because of her father. Her father had rented a home in Star Island long-term, though by the way the doctors were acting, long-term wasn't going to happen.

Blue rubbed his hand over his head again. *Fuck.* He hated that Mina was in there right now by herself. She'd been quiet on the ride over, simply holding his hand as they'd been driven by the armed team. But she'd basically closed in on herself.

He didn't blame her, but he still hated it. Hated seeing her in pain and not being able to comfort her.

This thing he felt for her, something he wouldn't put into words just yet because it terrified him, had come out of nowhere. And now he couldn't imagine her not in his life. Which was insane. He knew that. But it didn't change the fact that he'd fallen for her. *Hard.*

When he heard Harrison talking quietly into his radio, Blue's head jerked around, looking down the hall to the other side of the doorway where his boss stood with four others.

Harrison met his gaze and shook his head, as if to reassure him. "Just the exterior guys checking in. We're all clear."

Blue's tension eased a fraction, but he practically jumped when the door opened. After being in there for hours, Mina stepped out, her eyes swollen from crying. She opened her mouth once, then shook her head as she rushed into his arms. As he wrapped his arms around her, he glanced into the open doorway and saw one of the doctors pulling a sheet over her father's body. *Oh, shit.* When Harrison had made it clear Warren Hollingsworth had been close to death Blue hadn't imagined it was this close.

"Come on." He gathered her tight against him and led her down the hallway, ignoring everyone as he made his way to the room she'd taken when they first arrived. As he passed Harrison, he mouthed the word 'food', knowing his boss would understand. Even though she probably wouldn't feel like eating, Mina was going to need something to eat after the day she'd had and a lot of rest.

At the next hallway he steered her with him, keeping his arm tight around her shoulders. Even though she was tall, she felt so damn fragile against him as she tried to hold her sobs in.

"Just let it out," he murmured.

Another sob escaped as they reached her room, this one punching right through to his heart. Not caring what anyone thought, he lifted her into his arms. She didn't fight him, just buried her face against his neck and let loose the tears he knew she'd been holding in since she'd learned the news about her father back in Key West.

Without glancing back, he shut the bedroom door with his foot and headed for the curved settee in the corner of the massive room. Other than the bed it was the only piece of furniture big enough for him. Sitting down, he stretched out, keeping her close as she released all her pent up emotion. She burrowed into him, clutching onto his shirt as she cried. The way her body shook, her ragged tears, the almost palpable pain rolling off her, cut through him like a fifty cal. He just wanted to take all her agony away.

He wasn't sure how much time passed, but eventually she stilled against him. Even though her breathing steadied out he knew she wasn't sleeping.

She kept her head rested against his shoulder as she drew circles on his chest. "It was peaceful when he went," she said brokenly.

He tightened his grip, the sound of her teary voice raking against him like broken shards of glass. "I'm so sorry."

She sucked in a ragged breath. "Thank you. I hate that we lost this last year together. He...apologized for all our lost time, said I was the best daughter he could have asked for." She stopped abruptly, and he felt more wetness covering his neck as she silently cried. Eventually she continued, her voice stronger. "He wasn't exactly lucid near the end, but everything he said was what I've wanted to hear since I was a kid. I kind of love and hate him for that, for finally giving me all that, then leaving. I mean, I know he didn't leave of his own free will but still, why did he have to wait until he was dying?"

Blue knew she wasn't looking for an answer so he just held her.

She was silent again for a while, only shifting once to get more comfortable. He spread his legs wider, letting her snuggle up against him. He might hate the circumstances but he loved being able to comfort her. When she spoke again, her voice was utterly broken. "He…he had a dozen of my paintings surrounding him when he died. I didn't even know he'd bought them. He said they brought him comfort." She let out another sob, not as harsh as her first crying jag, but he knew she'd be mourning for a while.

This time when her breathing finally evened out he thought she'd fallen asleep. But when someone knocked softly on the door, she jerked against him and sat up. Her eyes were red-rimmed and glassy, the sight a knife to his gut.

"It's just food," he said quietly, rubbing his hand down her back. "Why don't you grab a hot shower and I'll set the food up for you. I'll get some clothes out too. You can eat then sleep." Her father had her room stocked with anything she could possibly want or need. It was clear her father had wanted her here with him at the end. Right now the only thing she needed was a full stomach and sleep.

"That sounds…really good." Her voice was raspy, but she pushed up from him and headed for the connecting bathroom on shaky legs.

As soon as she shut the door behind her, he opened the bedroom door and found Vincent on the other side holding a gym bag. Another one of the security team members held a silver tray with a silver domed top. Probably real silver too.

"We've got you clothes and enough food for both of you," Vincent said, handing him the bag.

"Thanks." He set the bag down and reached for the tray. It was probably over protective, but he didn't want anyone else in this room right now. Not even men he trusted. "In the morning she'll have a lot of stuff to deal with and I'm sure she'll let the team know what her plans are but for now, she's going to get some sleep." And he was going to make damn sure that happened. He glanced over his shoulder even though he knew she couldn't hear him, before looking at Vincent again. "If you find out anything about Ivan, call or text me." He wanted to be kept up to date on that situation even if he wasn't on the security detail anymore.

"Of course. We've got our guys patrolling the grounds, two are static near her bedroom window and we'll have a team stationed on each end of the hall," Vincent said.

Blue nodded, liking the setup, especially since he was also in the room with her and fully armed. He didn't care that the kidnappers had been caught, he wasn't letting his guard down until they knew everything about the plot to take her.

While waiting for Mina, Blue looked over the food they'd dropped off, then opened the bag Vincent had brought him. He was surprised to find his actual clothes. Vincent had an extra key to his place for emergencies so he must have sent someone over. He needed a shower, but that could wait until Mina was sound asleep. After changing into an old Marine Corps T-shirt and loose cotton jogging pants, he checked the security of the room again. He'd already done it when they'd arrived, but as he waited for her, he couldn't sit still.

As he was checking one of the windows again, the bathroom door opened. Steam billowed out behind Mina. Her hair was damp around her shoulders and she had a thick blue robe knotted around her slender waist.

He immediately crossed the room to her and experienced the strongest surge of protectiveness when she immediately went into his arms.

"The shower helped a little," she murmured against his chest. "I just keep thinking about everything I've got to do now. Talk to estate lawyers, deal with the funeral arrangements, and then there's Ivan—"

Blue leaned back and placed a finger over her lips. "You have nothing to worry about right now except eating and sleeping. In a few hours you can deal with all that but you're not going to be alone. I'll help you with everything."

She nodded, her shoulders relaxing as she glanced over at the tray. Almost on cue, her stomach rumbled and her cheeks flushed pink. The circumstances were wrong, but he loved it when she did that. "I didn't think I'd be hungry," she murmured.

"You've been through a lot. Your body needs the fuel now. And you'll sleep better." After a pause, he said, "I'm officially off your security detail." He wanted her to know that he wasn't going anywhere.

At that, her face fell and when tears welled up he froze. Shit, what had he said wrong?

Before he could ask her what had upset her, she said, "You're leaving?"

He swore savagely, taking them both by surprise, but he shook his head and tightened his grip on her hips. "I'm off the detail because my focus would be split. As long as you want me here, I'm not going anywhere. I'm going to help you with everything."

The tension that had bled into her expression immediately faded to be replaced by something he couldn't define. Almost a kind of wonder. "I don't know what I did to deserve you," she whispered.

That tightness in his throat was back. "I feel the same," he rasped out. He swallowed, feeling so out of his depth it was fucking terrifying. "When I left the Marines

I had no clue what I wanted to do. I just took this job with Red Stone because I was qualified and I liked the people I'd be working with. Now I feel like..." He scrubbed a hand over his face, feeling beyond raw as he tried to get the words out. "It sounds fucking stupid when I say it, but I feel like every decision I made, led me to meeting you." God, that was lame even if it was true.

To his surprise, Mina wrapped her arms around him in a tight hug, burying her face against his chest. "That's not stupid at all." Her words were slightly garbled against him, but he understood.

He felt as if he was in a freefall with her. Like he'd jumped out of a low-flying plane without a parachute. There was no safety net where she was concerned and he didn't give a shit. If he got burned by Mina, something told him it would be worth it.

CHAPTER TWELVE

Mina opened her eyes with a start, jerking upright in bed. As reality crashed in on her, sadness swelled through her as she thought about her father being gone. Then when she saw Alex's side of the bed empty, a pang of sadness sliced through her until she realized he was in the bathroom. She could faintly hear the sound of the shower running. Raking a hand through her hair, she glanced at the bedside clock. Two in the morning.

So she'd only slept a couple hours. It felt like a lifetime though. And she was famished. Sliding out of bed, she turned on the dim bedside lamp then took the dome top off the tray and set it aside. She could order more food because she knew her father had multiple chefs on site. Her father.

Her throat tightened as she replayed the final conversation they'd had. He'd been so open with her, so apologetic for making her feel like she was a disappointment. She hadn't even realized how much she'd craved hearing the words from him until last night. Now she had to plan his funeral and deal with so much financial stuff it made her head hurt.

Staring at the remnants of what she and Alex had eaten, she put the dome back on and took the tray to the door. She felt bad just leaving it for someone to get, but she didn't have the energy to take it to the kitchen and she didn't feel like searching for the kitchen in this strange house anyway.

As she closed the door behind her she heard the water shut off. Thoughts of a naked Alex with water rolling down that muscular chest, over his taut abdomen and even lower made her entire body tighten. The sharp realization that she was turned on stunned her. She hadn't thought she'd be able to feel anything but sadness right now. And this wasn't just about her wanting to find pleasure, she wanted a deeper connection with Alex. Before she could take a step back to the big bed, the door quietly opened and Alex stepped out—wearing only a towel around his trim waist.

When Alex saw her, his eyes widened. "Hey, I didn't mean to wake you."

"You didn't," she said, her gaze roaming hungrily over his bare chest.

Stepping out, he sort of wrapped his arms around his chest like he was trying to cover himself.

"Are you hiding yourself from me?" she asked, unable to stop the laughter from escaping. It seemed so ludicrous that he could possibly be doing that. Despite the last couple days and how raw she felt from losing her father, it felt strangely good to laugh.

She couldn't tell for sure because of the low lighting, but she guessed he might have flushed. He cleared his throat in that nervous way that always took her off guard. Everything about Alex screamed confidence but sometimes he seemed so insecure around her that it floored her.

His arms dropped from his chest. "No, I just didn't want you to think I was coming out here half-dressed for...other reasons."

"I wouldn't say no to those other reasons." The words just slipped out but she wasn't sorry she'd said them.

He stilled, his dark gaze pinning her with such heated intensity she felt it all the way to her toes. But just as quickly he looked away and grabbed his gym bag. "I forgot my bag out here," he muttered, taking a step away as if he was going to head right back into the bathroom.

"Are you just going to ignore what I said?" she asked quietly, sounding bolder than she felt.

He met her gaze again, but she couldn't read his expression. "Mina, you've been through a lot."

So had he. He'd had to freaking shoot someone, something she imagined was hard to deal with, even for someone trained like him. "And?"

He scrubbed a hand over his short hair, something he seemed to do when he was nervous. "And, I'm not taking advantage of you." Before she could respond, he practically sprinted to the bathroom, taking that bag with him.

She blinked at his ninja-like departure. She couldn't believe he thought he'd actually be taking advantage of her. For the first time in her life she knew without a doubt that a man wanted her simply for her. And not just any man. But Alex. A mouth-wateringly sexy giant of a man who'd already risked his life for her more than once in the past couple days since they'd met. Then he'd stayed on to take care of her after her father died.

After experiencing how talented he was with just his hands and mouth and feeling firsthand how thick his cock was, she knew without a doubt when they finally got completely naked together, it would be amazing between them. And she wasn't going to let his misguided idea of being noble get in the way. If she had to seduce him into it, she had no problem with that.

She wasn't sure how long he would be so she turned off the lamp then hurriedly stripped off her robe. She shoved it in the empty dresser drawer of the nightstand before sliding beneath the luxurious sheets and pulling them completely up to her shoulders. With her heart racing, she waited for him to return.

And waited. When fifteen minutes passed she wondered if he was going to stay in there the rest of the night. Thankfully the door cracked open a fraction, but before she got a good glimpse of him, he snapped the light off.

Even in the dimness she could see him as he made his way to the bed. He dropped his bag next to it, then quietly slid in next to her. She guessed by his careful movements that he thought she was asleep. Lying on his back, he let out what she thought sounded like a frustrated sigh. She hoped he was frustrated with himself and not her.

Sliding closer, she reached out a hand, stroking over his chest once. "Alex?"

"Yeah?" His voice was unsteady.

"Will you hold me?"

"Of course." He didn't even pause, just rolled over and pulled her into his arms.

And froze.

One of his big hands palmed her naked back as she cuddled up against his chest. His breathing hitched as he tentatively slid his hand lower down the curve of her spine, then lower still until he froze again right at the curve of her bare butt. The feel of his callused fingers on her skin sent a thrill of need through her, making her nipples tingle in awareness.

"You're naked." The words sounded accusing.

"You're very perceptive," she whispered against his chest, sliding her hand up under the hem of his shirt, teasing her fingers over the sharp lines and striations of his cut stomach.

"Mina..." He trailed off, as if he couldn't think of an argument.

Which was good because she didn't want to waste her time talking when they could be pleasuring each other. Pushing up, she moved quickly so that she was straddling him. With the light from the alarm clock and the faint light from behind the thick drapes covering the windows, she could make out his face. And she could tell he liked what he saw.

He drank in the sight of her naked and straddling him, his expression fierce. Like the warrior she knew him to be.

"Take off your shirt," she whispered, wanting to see him again.

Half leaning up, he stripped it off, then took her completely by surprise when he flipped them so that he was on top. He moved with such a liquid grace. Arching into him, she shuddered at the feel of her nipples brushing against his chest. The contact was electric and she loved the feel of his weight on her.

"You make me crazy," he murmured before brushing his mouth over hers. He cupped her head, tangling his fingers in her hair as he held her tight—as if he was afraid she'd change her mind.

No way in hell was that happening.

Unable to find any words, she wrapped her legs around him, needing that closeness. He still had cotton pants on, but they did nothing to hide his erection. Rolling her hips against him, she savored the feel of his thickness rubbing over her clit. Her nipples beaded even tighter as her inner walls clenched with an unfulfilled need.

With his free hand, he cupped one of her breasts, shuddering above her as he began lightly strumming her already sensitive nipple. Her core clenched again from the contact. Her heart pounded erratically and a rush of heat streaked through her as she imagined what he'd feel like pumping inside her. He'd barely touched her and she was ready to combust.

When he pulled his mouth away from hers she started to protest, but stilled when his dark eyes met hers. "Let me taste you first."

First, meaning before he… oh yeah, she was on board with that.

His hands stroked over her as he slowly kissed his way down her chest, across her breasts, along her stomach until finally he crouched between her legs. She wished the lights were on so she could see his expression clearly, but the sound of his erratic breathing told her that he was just as excited as she was.

Softly, he slid a finger down her damp slit. "You're so wet," he murmured, more to himself than to her as he bent down between her legs.

Yeah, she was, and getting wetter by the second. She struggled to keep her breathing calm as she waited for the touch of his mouth where she needed it the most.

With his thumbs, he spread her lower lips before gently stroking his tongue against her heat. Unable to stop her reaction, she jerked against his face. That was all it took for him to start teasing. He dipped a finger inside her as he began working her with his tongue. It was too much and too little at the same time.

He stroked and teased but never fully focused on her clit. And she had no doubt he was doing it intentionally.

She spread her legs wider as she slid her fingers through his short hair. Her touch seemed to affect him because he moaned against her. Taking her by surprise he slid his hands under her bent legs.

"Give me your hands," he said, lifting his face for only a moment.

Without thinking she did. He slid his fingers through hers, pressing her hands flat against the bed, his grip impossibly tight. It didn't hurt, but he was completely in charge. The knowledge got her even wetter.

As he held her hands down, he finally focused on her clit, his strokes the perfect pressure—and she realized why he'd wanted to hold her hands down. As he buried his face against her, mercilessly pleasuring her, she couldn't move, couldn't lessen the intensity of his teasing even if she'd wanted to.

On instinct she pulled against him. Each time she tugged, the harder he pressed against her bundle of nerves and the faster she raced toward climax. And he just kept thrashing her clit until finally her orgasm crashed into her, slamming out to all her nerve endings as she writhed against the sheets. Because of his hold, she could barely move, just arch her back at the onslaught of pleasure. Even when she thought she couldn't take anymore, when she started to tell him to stop, he pushed her into another climax.

"Alex!" Unable to stop herself from crying out, she didn't care who heard her. He hadn't even penetrated her, just used pure clitoral stimulation and she felt like she was in fucking heaven.

He made this growling/groaning sound against her, the sensation vibrating through her as she came down from her high. When he released her fingers, she didn't even attempt to move. Feeling boneless, she watched as he leaned over the bed. She heard the sound of a zipper. When he muttered, "Thank you, Vincent," she wondered what he meant until she saw him pull out a box of condoms.

Sitting up, she snagged it from him. He seemed stunned, but let her take it. As she ripped it open, he slid his pants off and she almost forgot to breathe. *Holy shit.* Her inner walls tightened again, that hunger building inside her worse than before. She should be sated after that intense climax, but right now she wanted more. So much more. She might have held him in her hands, stroked him to orgasm, but seeing how thick and long he was—she dropped the box.

Alex didn't miss a beat. He grabbed it and tore out one of the packets. She was glad he was doing it because she didn't trust her shaky hands.

In awe she watched as he rolled it over his erection— and was glad his hands shook too. She simply couldn't be the only one so affected.

Before she could tear her gaze away from the beautiful sight of his hand stroking down the length of his cock, he moved over her with that ninja quickness and crushed his mouth over hers. She moaned at the taste of herself on his lips, at his evident need. It shouldn't be so erotic, but damn it was.

She dug her fingers into his back as he guided himself to her opening. As his thickness started to penetrate her she realized he wasn't even using his hand. The man was so damn hard and she was soaking wet that it wasn't necessary. One of his hands cupped her breast as she reached around and grabbed his ass.

She pulled him into her, not wanting him to take his time. She just wanted to feel that thickness filling her.

But it was more than just physical. She wanted to hold him inside her, to be connected with him, to belong to him. As he buried himself balls deep, she moaned into his mouth at the stretching sensation. Letting her head fall back, her eyes closed as he started pumping into her. She could barely think as he thrust over and over, each time he slammed into her hitting that perfect spot designed to drive her crazy.

The harder he thrust, the more she realized she was going to come again. It shocked the hell out of her, but she embraced it. As she built closer and closer to another release she opened her eyes to find Alex watching her with such a hungry expression it pushed her over the edge.

She held his gaze, unable to look away as she climaxed, wanting him to see her at her most vulnerable. He'd given so much to her by just being himself that she wanted to give this to him. He meant so much to her already, it scared her.

As she let go, he did too, shouting her name as he found his own release. The tendons and muscles in his neck strained as he came until finally he buried his face against her neck, nuzzling her in the sweetest way as his thrusts slowed. Light shudders continued to overtake him until after what felt like an eternity he stilled, lifting his gaze to meet hers.

Smiling, she brushed her lips softly over his. "Thank you."

His eyebrows rose in confusion so she tightened her grip around him, digging her fingers into his back. "I don't mean for that—though thank you for two amazing orgasms—I just mean for being here, for being you." She didn't think she'd be able to get through any of this without him. That alone scared her because she'd never thought she'd want to depend on anyone. Now she realized that falling for someone didn't mean you depended on them in a needy way. It meant you found someone to support you and someone you supported right back. Someone you made sacrifices for and someone you couldn't imagine living without. That thought jarred her straight to her core.

He looked almost uncomfortable, or maybe confused, but he kissed her softly before slowly withdrawing from her. "Let me throw this away," he murmured before sliding off the bed.

She watched his butt tighten as he walked to the bathroom and as another rush of need swept through her, she knew that once with him would never be enough. And she planned to enjoy him to the fullest because deep down, she wasn't sure how long she'd have him in her life.

CHAPTER THIRTEEN

Blue's eyes snapped open, a surge of adrenaline rushing through him, but he remained still. Mina was stretched out over his chest sleeping soundly, her breathing steady, and his internal radar told him that dawn was breaking even before he looked at the clock. It also told him they weren't alone in the bedroom.

Not giving in to panic, he lowered his eyelids, hoping that whoever was in the room hadn't noticed he was awake. Something had registered in his subconscious, telling him they had an intruder, but he couldn't be sure who it was because the room was fairly silent. The ceiling fan made a muted sound above them, but other than that all was quiet.

There. A faint rustle near the closet. Letting his right hand slowly ease off the bed, he silently reached for the weapon he'd laid on the dresser.

"Don't even think about it," a male voice murmured an instant before light illuminated the room.

Damn it. He hadn't reached it and now he couldn't risk grabbing it. Blinking, it took Blue a few seconds to adjust. Almost immediately his gaze narrowed on a man he recognized from Hollingsworth's security team. The dark-haired man stepped from the shadows of the open closet, his free hand dropping from the Tiffany floor lamp he'd just turned on.

Wearing all black clothing, he was pointing his weapon—with a noise suppressor on the muzzle—directly at Blue. The man's green eyes were more manic than Blue had seen in some killers.

Blue pulled his hand back. "What are you doing?" he asked as Mina stirred. She'd been in a dead sleep so he wasn't surprised it was taking her this long to come to.

She shifted against him and made the sweetest purring sound. Out of the corner of his eye he watched her look up from his chest. She must have sensed something was wrong because she looked over her shoulder and yelped in alarm. Grabbing the sheet she tugged it over her breasts but remained glued to Blue's side. "What's going on?" she whispered, panic punctuating her words.

Right then, Blue wanted to kill this fucker.

"What's going on is, you're going to come with me right now," the man said. "You're going to transfer ten million dollars of your father's—your—money, and I'm going to leave. Simple as that. No one gets hurt." The man's words were quiet, guaranteeing he wouldn't be overheard. He likely wouldn't have been anyway. The insulation in this place was top of the line. He made a jerking motion with his weapon hand. "Get dressed, both of you. And if you make a move toward your gun,

I'll shoot her in the stomach," the man said, his gaze pinning Blue's.

Blue could see the truth in the other man's eyes. He was desperate and would do it.

"We're going to do what he says. I'll get your clothes," Blue murmured to Mina. As he started to slide out of bed, he heard his phone buzzing across the dresser with a text alert.

The other man jerked once, but didn't say anything. Blue knew he couldn't look at it so he ignored the alert and dragged on his pants while keeping an eye on the guy. Then he grabbed one of his T-shirts and handed it to Mina without looking at her. When he went to grab a pair of his pants for her, the man shook his head. "The shirt is fine," he growled.

Even with her height it would fall to mid-thigh, but Blue didn't want her so exposed, knowing it would add to her sense of vulnerability. Right now he couldn't stand to see the fear he knew was etched on her face. He had to stay focused because he was going to get her out of this.

The man reached into his back pocket and tossed flex cuffs onto the bed, still keeping a solid fifteen feet between them. There was no way for Blue to rush the guy. He'd be shot before he made it a couple feet.

"Cuff your boyfriend to the headboard. You're coming with me."

154 | KATIE REUS

Hell, no. Blue wasn't letting her go anywhere. Mina slid off the bed and gave Blue an apologetic look as she stood next to him.

Blue stepped forward, putting his body half in front of hers. "I go where she goes," he said. Because he knew that the second he was cuffed, the man would shoot him anyway. Blue could see it in the guy's eyes. He just wanted to give Mina the illusion of a choice to keep her docile. Because there was no way in hell this man would leave Blue behind to alert the team that Mina had been taken.

Mina must have come to the same conclusion because she stepped up beside him. "He comes with me. You could shoot him, but it would be a very stupid choice. Because you'll have to shoot me or drag me kicking and screaming with you if you do. And I don't think you want that. You just want your money. I'm willing to give it to you for our lives. Are you willing to kill us and get nothing? Because I swear if you hurt him, you will not only get nothing, you'll end up dead by the security team in this house." Her voice was so damn calm, so resolute, silence reigned in the room for a long moment.

Blue was so damn proud of her. He'd seen grown men lose their shit when staring down the barrel of a loaded weapon. Not Mina.

The man—Jesse Rendon, the name finally clicked into place from one of the files Blue had read—glared at

Mina, his jaw tight. Finally he gave a sharp nod. "Fine, he comes with us. But you cuff his hands behind his back."

By the subtle shift of her feet, the aggressive stance, Blue could tell she wanted to argue, but he nodded. "That's fine. Cuff me, Mina." Even if his hands were secured, he could use the rest of his body as a weapon. He just needed to get close enough and wait for the right opening. He turned to the side so the man could see her do it. He tensed his muscles, making his wrists slightly thicker as she put them in place. It was a trick used to get out of metal handcuffs, but it likely wouldn't work with flex cuffs. Still, he had to try something.

"I'm sorry, Alex," she whispered.

"Don't be. We're going to get through this." Blue's phone buzzed again, but he ignored it as he watched Rendon. "Jesse doesn't want to hurt us, do you?" he asked the man, intentionally using his name. It was a small way to humanize the situation, and even though Blue knew it would do little to stop this guy from killing them, he was going to use everything he had available in his arsenal to get them out of this.

Wariness flickered across the man's face. But he didn't respond. Just stepped back from the opening of the closet and motioned them in. "You go first," he said to Blue. "I'll keep the gun on your girl. You try anything, I'll shoot her in the spine."

Ice slithered through Blue's veins, hating this bastard more than he'd hated anyone. As he took a few steps forward, ready to take the lead in what he guessed was a hidden walkway of sorts, there was a sharp knock on the door before it started to open.

Rendon turned, likely on instinct, and when he did, moved his weapon off Mina and Blue. Knowing it might be the only chance he got, Blue rushed forward on a burst of pure energy. He bent and rammed his shoulder into the guy's chest.

Rendon shouted in pain as he slammed back against the wall. But he didn't lose his weapon. As he started to raise it, Blue hauled back, ready to slam into him again. He'd use every available body part to keep this guy down.

Before he'd taken a step, something flew by him. A vase smashed into Rendon's face. He screamed when his head snapped back. As he dropped the weapon, Blue rammed him again, using his shoulder to pin him to the wall. It felt like a damn eternity had passed, but he knew only seconds had ticked by as the Red Stone team poured into the room.

As Rendon slumped against the wall, moaning in pain and holding his face, Vincent grabbed the man, flipped him over and secured his hands behind his back. Once Blue was sure the man was down, he turned to Mina and rushed to her. Even though he couldn't hold her, she wrapped her arms around his neck and held tight.

She buried her face against him, her grip fierce and protective. "I thought I'd lose you," she said on a sob.

"No way in hell." Before he could turn to ask someone to cut him free, a hand landed on his wrist.

"Don't move," Harrison said.

A second later his hands were loose and he pulled Mina tight against him. Keeping her close, Blue turned to view the madhouse of their room. Vincent and another man were hauling Rendon from the room, but Blue kept his focus on Harrison. "What the hell is going on?"

"One of the kidnappers in Key West flipped on Rendon to make a deal. Told the police that he was their contact, not Ivan Mitchell. Looks like Rendon set Mitchell up, using the other man's phone to make some of his phone calls. When we went to retrieve Rendon, he wasn't in his room. And when you didn't answer your texts, we thought something might be wrong," Harrison said.

"Secret fucking tunnel!" Grant shouted from the closet, drawing their attention to him as he stepped out of the walk-in closet. The former detective looked pissed. "The entrance is seamless. It's not on the house plans but we should have known about this."

Yeah, no shit. Blue turned to look at Mina. "You okay?" he murmured.

Face pale, she nodded and tightened her grip around his waist before looking at Harrison. "Is this over now? Are there possibly more people involved?"

Harrison shook his head, his expression dark. "Not that we know of. But I recommend you let your father's security team go and replace them. It doesn't have to be with Red Stone, but you should start fresh."

Without pause, she nodded. "With the exception of Ivan, I want everyone gone. I don't know any of these guys anyway. They were only with my dad the last year. I'll give them all generous severance packages, but I want them gone now. As in right now. Can you guys make that happen?" She sounded so fucking exhausted Blue wanted to take her somewhere insulated from the world even though he knew that wasn't possible.

Harrison smiled, though it looked like more of a baring of his teeth, as if he couldn't wait to get rid of the other team—probably because of the secret entrance oversight. "Consider it done. Mitchell will be here within the hour and I'm sure you'll have a lot to go over with him." He looked at Blue. "A couple detectives from Key West PD are coming up too and they want to talk to both of you. In light of what's happened with Miss Hollingsworth, they're making an exception and letting you both make your statement here."

Thank God. Blue nodded. "What about Rendon?"

Harrison shrugged. "We'll let Miami PD and Key West PD figure out who gets to take him in. Personally I don't give a shit. I just want him gone."

"Me too," Mina muttered.

Harrison gave her a polite nod, then jerked his head that he wanted a moment alone with Blue. Though he didn't want to let Mina go even for a second, Blue squeezed her shoulders and she stepped out of his embrace. "I'm going to change in the bathroom anyway," she murmured, giving him and Harrison privacy.

"What is it?"

"I know you've got a lot of shit to deal with over the next week, but once the dust has settled, I want a private sit-down with you Monday. Not tomorrow, next Monday," he added, when Blue was about to tell him that tomorrow would never work.

"Are you firing me?" he asked, wanting to know now.

Taking him by surprise, Harrison grinned. "No. I've got business I want to discuss, but it can wait. You need to take care of your woman. If you need longer than a week, let me know. I won't be on this detail after today but the team I'm sending in is the best. If you have any specific requests, just tell me."

Blue shook his head. Red Stone only hired the best anyway. Whoever Harrison chose was fine with him. "I trust your judgment."

Seeming pleased by that, Harrison nodded before turning and getting into a conversation with one of the team members. Blue immediately headed for the bathroom. After he knocked and announced himself, Mina pulled the door open only enough to let him in.

Needing to feel her in his arms, he held her close. "That was an impressive throw," he said, hoping to ease some of the tension on her face.

She smiled, letting out a startled laugh. "I'm just sorry I didn't do more damage to that bastard. I'm almost afraid to believe it's all really over."

"Believe it, sweetheart. No one is ever going to get to you like that again." And he was going to make damn sure they suffered if they tried. "But...now that your father is gone, you're going to have to think about stronger security measures. It doesn't matter how low-key of a life you live. And I know this was an inside job, but eventually, someone will figure out how wealthy you are and come after you again. We can make it so that you're not living in a prison, but you're going to need a security detail more often than not." He felt strange giving advice like this when he didn't even know how to define their relationship, but it needed to be said.

"We?" she asked softly and he realized what he'd said.

"You."

She frowned. "I like the sound of we better."

"Thank God. Mina...this thing between us. I've never felt anything like it before." Hell, he sounded like an idiot.

"Me neither. And I feel stupid saying this, but I hope you know that I want more than just sex. I want a relationship, to see where this thing goes, to spend all my freaking free time with you and—"

Blue crushed his mouth over hers, needing to taste her like he needed his next breath. He didn't have all the answers about their future, but he knew his future included Mina in it.

CHAPTER FOURTEEN

One week later

Blue nodded at Lizzy, who was Harrison's personal assistant/computer guru, clacking away on her keyboard as he entered her private office. She immediately stopped what she was doing when she saw him. Her office was the final barrier to Harrison's and Blue had just gotten the go-ahead from one of the assistants in the exterior office to come in here. "Go on in," Lizzy said, motioning behind her to the closed door. "They're waiting for you."

They? He wasn't sure who she was referring to other than Harrison, but didn't ask. He'd had a long week helping Mina deal with her father's funeral and just being there for her emotionally. He wouldn't want to be anywhere else, but seeing Mina in pain killed him and right now he didn't relish the idea of getting ambushed. Harrison had been tight-lipped regarding what this meeting was about so Blue just nodded and murmured thanks to Lizzy before heading in.

Harrison and Porter were sitting in two chairs on the side of the desk closest to him. And there was a third chair in front of them. He frowned, wondering why the hell Harrison wasn't sitting at his chair, and why his brother Porter was here.

"Hey, guys."

Harrison smiled and motioned to the empty chair. "It's a crazy week and all the conference rooms are in use. Figured it'd be easier to just meet here anyway. How's Mina?"

Blue sat, still wondering what the hell this was all about. "Hanging in there." She was at his place now, where she'd been staying the last week. They hadn't discussed her going back to Key West and truthfully, it was something he didn't want to even think about. He knew it was too soon to ask but he wanted her living with him permanently. "What's going on, guys?"

Harrison shot Porter an unreadable look. Porter just shrugged in that stoic way of his. "Be blunt," he said, as if answering a question.

Harrison gave a shrug and looked back at Blue. "We're going to be upfront with you, but first, what are your intentions with Mina Hollingsworth?"

He bristled. "How the fuck is that any of your business?" He wasn't going to answer any questions about his personal life, especially when he hadn't broached the subject of the future with Mina yet.

To his surprise, Harrison actually smiled. "What I should have asked was, would you prefer to be stationed in Miami on a permanent basis? Very limited travel."

"Yes." He didn't even have to think about it.

"Good. Porter and I talked about this with our dad and even though he's taking a backseat to business lately, he's on board...We'd like to put you in charge of one of our East Coast divisions. It would include the Hollingsworth account, unless Mina is disagreeable. But I don't see that happening. You can keep a pulse on her security in addition to the others in your division, you'll be local, and we won't lose you."

Blue sat there a moment, absorbing everything. "Lose me?"

Harrison nodded. "Look, I know how much you're worth. I've never mentioned it because I didn't see a reason to. I figured if you wanted to work here when you don't even need a job, you had your reasons, but with your net worth and your track record of investments, we want you as part of our team in a broader capacity. Now that you're with Mina, something tells me the prospect of traveling when you don't need to will eventually drive you to quit. We don't want that."

Blue rubbed a hand over his face, stunned by the offer. "How'd you know about my financials?"

Harrison gave him a wry look. "Seriously? With the background checks we run, we know everything we need to about our employees."

Yeah, he'd figured. "Okay, what exactly does this entail? Is it contingent on the Hollingsworth account?"

Harrison shook his head. "Nope. This offer was coming by the end of the year. Your relationship with her just moved it up. You're more than qualified. In fact, I'd say you're uniquely qualified."

Wordlessly Porter handed him a folded piece of paper. When Blue opened it he read an outline of his potential duties—a lot more management stuff, which worked well for all his experience as an officer—and his new salary and benefits. It was impressive. And much more up his alley. Until Mina he'd felt so damn lost, like he was going through the motions. Now this offer? It seemed too good to be true. "I need to think about it, but I can let you know by tomorrow." And talk to Mina. He was going to lay all his cards on the table tonight and might as well tell her about this too.

Harrison nodded, as if he'd expected it. "Take your time."

After talking details for a few more minutes, Blue said his goodbyes to both men, feeling completely stunned. On the way back to his place he stopped at a local florist and picked up a bouquet of tulips since Mina loved them. He barely remembered the drive to his high-rise condo. Once he made it to the penthouse floor he was relieved to see the security team still standing guard. Not that he doubted them, but leaving Mina for even an hour felt like too much now. He knew that would fade in time once he trusted that she was no longer a target, but his need to protect her never would.

As he entered his place he heard muted voices coming from the direction of the living room. Mina's and Ivan's. Blue gritted his teeth, not liking that the other man was here. Ivan was protective of Mina and while Blue appreciated it, he was big enough to admit he didn't like the camaraderie between the two of them. It was archaic and a little juvenile, but he wasn't going to deny his feelings when it came to Mina. He loved her. There wasn't a doubt in his mind.

When he stepped into the living room, he was once again reminded of how damn right Mina looked in his place. Sitting on one of his couches wearing one of those flowy summer dresses, her feet tucked under her as she sipped a glass of white wine, the bright lights of the city behind her through the floor to ceiling windows, she looked like home to him.

It was the only way he could describe her. Being with her, coming back to her every night, *was* home. She smiled broadly when she saw him and when her gaze landed on the flowers, she actually flushed pink, clearly pleased. And it made him feel ten feet tall.

"Hey, sweetheart," he murmured, covering the distance across the hardwood floor in seconds. Before she could rise, he'd taken his place next to her, brushing his lips over hers in a way he meant to be possessive because Ivan was there.

Laughing lightly, because she likely knew what he was doing, she pushed at his chest. "Ivan just stopped by to talk to us."

Us? More like Mina. Probably wanted to convince her to dump Blue. He'd seen the way the other man looked at him and was well aware Ivan didn't think he was good enough for her. Well, fuck him.

Blue set the flowers on the table next to her wine then looked at Ivan, keeping his expression blank. "Interesting timing. Did you intentionally plan to stop by when you knew I'd be gone?"

"I did." The truth of his statement took Blue off guard. Before he could respond, Ivan continued. "But not for the reasons you think. I haven't been here long so I haven't had a chance to tell Mina everything. And I'm not going to sugarcoat any of this. I had you thoroughly checked out. If I didn't, I'd be terrible at my job. You saved Mina more than once and no one could ever doubt your honor, but I still had to be sure about you." He cleared his throat, looking nervous as he flicked a glance at Mina.

Blue looked down at her to find her lips pulled into a thin line, but she didn't seem surprised. And if he was being honest, Blue would have lost respect for the guy if he hadn't checked him out. "And?"

"And...I know you're not after Mina for her money." He pointed at a thick manila file on the glass-topped coffee table. "From our brief discussions about you, it doesn't sound like you've told her as much as you should about yourself. I never thought anyone would be good enough for her, but God, you're like an all-American hero," he muttered in mock-disgust, drawing out a small smile from Blue. "Give me a call tomorrow. I know what your meeting with the Caldwell brothers was about so once you've made a decision, we need to talk specifics if you're going to be in charge of..." He trailed off, standing. "Just call me."

Blue was surprised the other man knew about it, but maybe he shouldn't be. It wasn't surprising Harrison would have told Ivan, especially if Blue was going to head up Mina's security detail—which Ivan currently led. Even though Ivan didn't work for Red Stone, Blue had a feeling that was going to change soon. He wanted to offer the man a job and make his position permanent. His loyalty for the woman Blue loved was unquestionable so even if the guy rubbed him the wrong way sometimes, he didn't care. Mina's safety was more important than anything.

Mina nudged Blue in the side. "Are either of you going to tell me what you're talking about?"

He squeezed her shoulder. "Yeah, in just a minute."

Taking the cue, Ivan headed for the door. "I'll let myself out."

When Mina went to get up to walk him out, Blue tightened his grip around her shoulders. "He's fine."

She gave him an annoyed look, but didn't argue. Just nestled closer to him until he pulled her onto his lap. "All right, start talking. What was all that about?" she asked as soon as Ivan was gone.

"Maybe you should just read the file."

She tweaked his nose, making him smile, something he did more and more every day. "Or maybe you should just tell me what's in it."

"Before I joined the Marines you know I played pro ball." When she nodded, he continued. "I received a healthy signing bonus—very healthy. I barely touched it, instead I worked with a couple financial advisors and I've got a little over ten million in the bank."

Her eyes widened. "Are you serious?"

He nodded. "Yep."

"Okay, so you're definitely not after me for my money," she said teasingly.

Blue slid a hand up under her long dress, skimming along her smooth legs, up her inner thigh until he cupped her mound. Her *bare* mound. "This is what I want from you," he said, his voice raspy.

"I hope that's not *all* you want." She sounded just as unsteady as he felt and when he tweaked her clit, she shuddered.

He shook his head, stilling his hand. "Definitely not. I know it's too soon and I argued with myself the entire way here, but, shit, okay, I'm just going to say it."

"I love you, Alex." Mina bit her bottom lip, her green eyes nervous as she watched him.

Her words rolled over him, wrapping around him like a warm embrace, making it impossible for him to think. He hadn't known how much he'd wanted her to say that until now.

"Say something," she whispered, and he realized he'd just been staring. Because he was stunned that this sweet, smart, beautiful woman loved him too.

She shifted against his lap. "It's okay if you don't. The last couple weeks have made me realize that life is too short to hold back anything and I just wanted you to know." But he could hear the nervousness in her voice

He mentally shook himself, feeling like a jackass for just sitting here. "I love you too. So fucking much. More than I ever imagined possible, Mina. I want you to move in with me. I've got more than enough space, and we can make any of the rooms your studio. Hell, we can knock down a wall and make you a giant studio." Anything to make her happy. "But if you want to live in Key West, that's fine too. I'll move there with you—if you'll have me." He'd tell her about his new job offer later. He didn't want to affect her decision or for her to think he was trying to use his job offer as a guilt tactic or something. Because he would give it up if she wanted him to move with her.

"Yes." She smiled widely, her happiness clear as she shifted positions and straddled him.

He immediately pushed her dress up to her thighs, stroking his hands up and down her bare legs. He loved simply touching her. "Yes? Just like that?"

She lifted a dark eyebrow. "You want me to argue?"

Throat tight, he shook his head. "No, I just thought I might have to convince you a little harder."

At that, her eyes gleamed wickedly. "What kind of method were you planning to use to *convince* me?"

He cupped her mound again, sliding a finger inside her this time, pleased to find her already wet. "How about I show you?"

Letting out a soft moan as he pushed another finger inside her tight sheath, she shakily nodded. "I like the sound of that."

He planned to show her that he was the man for her every day for the rest of their lives.

ACKNOWLEDGMENTS

I owe a big thanks to Kari Walker, Laura Wright and Joan Turner for their insight with this story. Thank you ladies for everything. For my readers, thank you again for loving this series. I'm constantly amazed by how you not only read my books, but spread the word about them and I'm truly grateful. As always, thank you to Tanya Hyatt, who does so many behind the scenes things so I can focus on writing. Last, but never least, I'm thankful to God.

COMPLETE BOOKLIST

Red Stone Security Series
No One to Trust
Danger Next Door
Fatal Deception
Miami, Mistletoe & Murder
His to Protect
Breaking Her Rules
Protecting His Witness
Sinful Seduction

The Serafina: Sin City Series
First Surrender
Sensual Surrender
Sweetest Surrender

Deadly Ops Series
Targeted
Bound to Danger (2014)

Non-series Romantic Suspense
Running From the Past
Everything to Lose
Dangerous Deception

Dangerous Secrets
Killer Secrets
Deadly Obsession
Danger in Paradise
His Secret Past

Paranormal Romance
Destined Mate
Protector's Mate
A Jaguar's Kiss
Tempting the Jaguar
Enemy Mine
Heart of the Jaguar

Moon Shifter Series
Alpha Instinct
Lover's Instinct (novella)
Primal Possession
Mating Instinct
His Untamed Desire (novella)
Avenger's Heat

Darkness Series
Darkness Awakened
Taste of Darkness (2014)

ABOUT THE AUTHOR

Katie Reus is the *New York Times* and *USA Today* bestselling author of the Red Stone Security series, the Moon Shifter series and the Deadly Ops series. She fell in love with romance at a young age thanks to books she pilfered from her mom's stash. Years later she loves reading romance almost as much as she loves writing it.

However, she didn't always know she wanted to be a writer. After changing majors many times, she finally graduated summa cum laude with a degree in psychology. Not long after that she discovered a new love. Writing. She now spends her days writing dark paranormal romance and sexy romantic suspense. For more information on Katie please visit her website: www.katiereus.com. Also find her on twitter @katiereus or visit her on facebook at: www.facebook.com/katiereusauthor.

21942360R00108

Made in the USA
Middletown, DE
15 July 2015